WITH
DUDLE

D1325470

Aces Wild

They were an odd pair, the one-time Union captain and the former Confederate sergeant. They'd fought each other during the Battle of Pea Ridge . . . and then ended up fighting shoulder to shoulder when a common enemy showed his face.

Bo Rangle, leader of the guerilla force known as Rangle's Raiders, took advantage of the slaughter to steal what the two opposing forces had been fighting for – two hundred thousand dollars' worth of Confederate gold.

Hank Brazos and Duke Benedict never forgot that day, or each other. And when, by chance, their trails crossed again after the War, they decided to team up, find Rangle and reclaim that gold for themselves. And while they were at it, they swore to get revenge for all of their comrades who'd died that day back in 1862. . . .

Aces Wild

E. Jefferson Clay

ROBERT HALE

First published by Cleveland Publishing Co. Pty Ltd,
New South Wales, Australia
First published in 1967

ISBN 978-0-7198-3081-5

The Crowood Press
The Stable Block
Crowood Lane
Ramsbury
Marlborough
Wiltshire SN8 2HR

www.bhwesterns.com

Robert Hale is an imprint
of The Crowood Press

ONE

BENEDICT'S FULL HAND

'All right, Benedict, what have you got?'

'Pardon?'

'I said what are you holdin', dammit, I'm callin'.'

Duke Benedict grinned as he came back to earth and spread his cards face-up on the green baize. 'Full house.'

It was yet another winning hand and faces darkened around the table. To be good-looking, well-dressed and a smooth talker all in one stranger was enough to rile the Bird Cage's hardcase poker players anytime, without him starting in on a lucky streak to boot. Worse, he was still able to win with his mind plainly on other things, like a pair of silk-stockinged legs across the room. It was enough to make a saint start cursing.

Liveryman Buck Tanner was no saint, but he knew how to curse. He gave a lurid demonstration, then snapped:

'You sure we ain't borin' you, Benedict?' Buck's rough

voice was heavily laced with sarcasm. He was down fifty bucks.

'Yeah, we ain't keepin' you from nothin', are we?' cowboy Flory Rand chimed in, eighty dollars behind, and already on the Bird Cage's slate for drinks.

Duke Benedict heard the voices but not the words – a picture of lazy grace as he absently raked in the latest pot. He went on gazing across the room, with a sparkle in his clear gray eyes. Those legs were enough to make a man forget his religion if he was still lucky enough to have any religion left in him in Daybreak, Kansas, he reflected.

The feet were very small, he noted with an expert eye. He'd heard that small feet indicated fine breeding. Was she highly bred? He seriously doubted it. Nobody of breeding would be found dead in the Bird Cage Saloon – except himself of course, and he was anything but dead.

His eyes left the ankles and moved upwards. The crossed, silky-smooth calves were so perfect that they immediately reminded him of Glory LaRue and the Golden Gate Gambling Hall, Dallas, Texas.

He and Glory had had a fine old time down there in Dallas before the War of the States had ripped America apart, and just thinking of Glory and how she kicked those long slim legs set his mind to wandering. Leaning back in his chair, he puffed reflectively on his black cigar and a small smile played at the corners of his handsome mouth.

That smile clinched it for Big Henry Peck, heaviest loser of the three, and as Daybreak's rugged blacksmith, the least charmed by the gambling man's looks, manners, and winning ways.

'Goddamn tinhorn,' the big man muttered as he picked up his fresh cards. Then, emboldened by Benedict's absent gaze, he added, 'Yankee son-of-a-bitch.'

Any way you looked at it, it was Big Henry's unlucky day all around. Not only had he lost the best part of twenty-five dollars, but Benedict heard him. The cigar swung to point at the blacksmith like a gun barrel. Behind it, Benedict was smiling, but the smile was anything but friendly.

'How's that again, blacksmith?'

'You heard.'

'I'd like you to repeat it.'

Big Henry glared. The big blacksmith was a brawler of wide repute and to him, Duke Benedict was just a dude who'd ridden into Daybreak two days ago and since then had alternated his time between playing cards at the Bird Cage or the Shotgun, and visiting Belle Shilleen's sporting house on the corner of Piute and Johnny Streets.

Benedict had caused plenty of interest around Daybreak, particularly among the womenfolk, but nobody knew how he rated, if he rated at all.

Maybe now was the time to find out, Big Henry decided, glancing about him. Tanner and Rand were bound to back him, he figured, and just a couple of tables away saloonkeeper Harp Moody and his bouncers Beecher and Quade were drinking together. Over by the west wall, Joe Crook sat in his permanent place on the high stool six feet above the Bird Cage's customers, with his double-barreled Richardson shotgun lying across his knees. Big Henry grinned. He and Joe Crook were good pards.

Yeah, maybe now was the right time to find out what the gambling man was made of.

The smith flexed his huge muscles and his lips twisted into a sneer.

'What I said, Benedict, is that you're a son-of-a-bitch.'

Benedict's smile widened. The gray eyes went over Tanner and Rand, then to Moody's table, then up to the shotgun. The gambler wondered just how far Joe Crook would leave a ruckus go before cutting loose.

The saloon quietened suddenly as Benedict rose to his feet. Henry Peck immediately jumped up, knocking over his chair. Benedict inhaled deeply on his cigar, then carefully stubbed it out.

Rand and Tanner remained seated, but their expressions left no doubt whose side they were on.

Duke Benedict shot his cuffs, straightened his hat and glanced to his right. The owner of the lovely legs was watching him with lively interest. That was all the encouragement Duke Benedict needed.

Things were going too slowly for Big Henry. 'All right, tinhorn,' he challenged, flexing some more. 'I called you a son-of-a-bitch. So what are you goin' to do about it?'

Benedict quickly showed him. With one flashing motion he seized the poker table and slammed Big Henry in the face with it, chips, money and glassware spilling in wild confusion.

Tanner and Rand jumped from their chairs as Benedict came around the wrecked table with six-guns leaping into his hands as if by some gambler's sleight-of-hand trick. A gun blurred and the bloody-nosed Big Henry buckled and fell. Benedict stepped lightly past the crumpling big figure and hit Buck Tanner with all his force, splitting his forehead from eyebrow to hairline and knocking him a full six feet to crash into Harp Moody's table and send it flying.

Startled by the speed of the attack, young cowboy Flory Rand nevertheless had his six-gun half clear by the time Benedict swung his attention to him. A highly-polished boot flashed out. Rand's gun was spilled to the floor and then a venomous whack from Benedict's pearl-handled six-gun sent him after it.

It was all over in seconds. Stepping back from the scene of carnage, Benedict twirled his six-guns on his fingers and put a big smile on his face for the benefit of choleric Harp Moody as he let the Colts drop back into their holsters. Moody, advancing menacingly with Beecher and Quade, saw the guns go back to leather and halted uncertainly in the face of that smile.

'No hard feelings, Moody,' Benedict said, friendly as hell. 'Just a friendly argument.' He looked reproachfully down at the sleeping Peck. 'He hard-named my mother.' A murmur of approval went around the saloon. All of the Bird Cage's customers had mothers. One or two could even remember them.

Harp Moody reflected the general feeling. 'That just wasn't perlite. Beecher, Quade, toss a bucket of water over these boys.'

The bouncers obeyed smartly, voices rose again and the tension washed away. Harp Moody signaled to Joe Crook to take the shotgun off the cock, then crossed to the bar and stood with a drink in his fist, looking speculatively across the room at the man who'd whipped Peck and the others, yet still didn't have a hair out of place.

The stares of a hundred Harp Moodys would have had less than no effect on Duke Benedict at that moment, for he was now seated with the owner of the legs at her table. If the gambler had a real weakness you could put a finger on, it was a weakness for the opposite sex, and this was as stirring a representative of that fair gender as he'd encountered in Daybreak. She was small and dark, with a pert high-breasted figure, rounded hips, and a way of fluttering her long dark eyelashes that gave Benedict the old familiar tingling under the skin.

She told him she thought he was very brave and masterful, the way he'd handled Peck and company who by now had been dragged out back to recuperate. Benedict didn't argue. Nor did she when he told her that she had eyes like a Spanish queen. They were getting along marvelously.

Things eventually came down to earth a little however when Benedict noticed the rings on her left hand. Yes, she admitted a little glumly, she was married. Her name was Honey Smith and she was married to one Surprising Smith. They'd arrived in Daybreak just that morning.

'Surprising Smith?' said Benedict. 'That's some name, Honey. Tell me, what brings you to Daybreak?' Honey sighed, the deep breath doing interesting things to the low-cut front of her dress. 'My husband is a bounty-hunter. He has been hired by the Daybreak town council to assist the deputy run down some local badmen.' She pulled a pretty face. 'Now I suppose you won't want to sit with me?'

'I wouldn't say that,' Benedict said staunchly, though

privately wondering why all the most desirable ones seemed to have the most formidable husbands. Then curiously, 'But where did he get that handle? What's surprising about him?'

Honey Smith's pout suggested that she found her husband a rather boring topic of conversation. 'Oh, it's some silly name the outlaws gave him because he is always taking them by surprise. He's very successful at his work,' she added grudgingly, leaving no doubt in Benedict's mind that she disapproved of her husband's occupation. Then she brightened and dimpled charmingly. 'But let's talk about something more interesting, Duke. Let's talk about you.'

Benedict was only too ready to oblige. Ordering drinks, he launched into an engaging, if not particularly truthful account of his life. Honey was fascinated and within a mere matter of minutes Mr Surprising Smith was totally forgotten by both and might have remained so indefinitely, if the batwings hadn't suddenly squeaked open causing Honey to stiffen and interrupt Benedict's monologue with a startled cry.

'My husband!'

To Duke Benedict, it seemed that many of the best moments of his life had been ruined by somebody suddenly saying: 'My husband!'

He sighed, tugged down the lapels of his immaculate coat, then rose as Surprising Smith advanced, looking surprisingly menacing.

Pretty Honey's husband was a slender man of less than average height who held himself stiffly erect to appear taller. He was dressed entirely in black with a gun thonged low on each lean thigh. His sour face was darkly narrow, ornamented by a black dash of a moustache, the eyes pale. As he drew up at the table, he had, for Benedict, all the appeal of a copperhead.

'Get up!' Surprising Smith said to his wife.

Honey got up. Quickly.

'Now, darlin', don't go jumping to conclusions. I was only—'

'Half-an-hour is all I leave you for, and that's all the lousy time it takes for you to get up to your old tricks, pickin' up the first thing in pants you meet.'

'No, no that's not at all the way it is, Mr er . . . Surprising sir,' Benedict smiled. He put everything into that smile for the little gunfighter looked touchy as a teased snake. 'You see, your lady wife and I were simply enjoying a sociable.

'You just ain't to be trusted,' Smith went on to his wife as if Benedict hadn't spoken. He seized her wrist and jerked her roughly to him, upsetting her chair. 'You flighty little vixen. How many times I got to hammer you to . . . .'

'Take it easy, Smith,' Benedict cut in, no longer smiling.

'. . . teach you that you ain't to drink with other men? You ain't to talk to 'em, you ain't even to—'

Benedict's right boot flashed and Surprising Smith jolted from head to toe as the kick connected with his backside.

'You need a lesson in manners, friend,' Benedict snapped as the little man released his wife and spun to face him squarely, his face now an ugly mask. 'This might be a rough old town, but it's not that rough.'

Surprising Smith sucked in a ragged breath, his fingers wriggling over his gun butts like little snakes.

'You shouldn't have done that – now go for iron, you philanderin', white-fingered, pantywaist tinhorn!'

Honey Smith gave a little shriek of dismay. Duke Benedict's face went cold and hard, but before he could speak, the explosive quiet was broken by the unmistakable click of a shotgun hammer going back.

'All right, boys,' Joe Crook said from his high chair, peering down at them over the sights of the Richardson. 'Jest you back up there, 'less you want a load of buckshot apiece.'

Neither man moved; a man would have to be six kinds of a fool to do otherwise. Harp Moody came across from the bar. Moody, who'd signaled to Crook to get the drop as soon as he smelt gunplay, had his hands in his pockets so they wouldn't see them trembling. But his voice was firm enough.

Slowly Smith let his hands drop to his sides. Benedict eased his pent-up breath slowly out. Then Harp Moody was standing between him and Surprising Smith.

'All right, Benedict, out!'

Benedict looked indignant. 'Who, me? Why not him?'

'On account it ain't him that's been bustin' up my saloon and it ain't him that's been shinin' up to other fellers' wives,' Moody explained. He snapped his fingers and immediately Beecher and Quade moved in and grabbed the gambler's arms.

'Shotgun's on you, Benedict,' warned Moody. 'Go peaceable or you're daid.'

Benedict sighed but didn't argue. Not with that riot gun on him. With a regretful look at Honey he let them walk him fast to the doors.

Benedict went so peaceable, his handlers mistook caution for cowardice and put a little extra muscle into their work for the benefit of the spectators as they neared the batwings. Benedict retaliated by slamming a heel into big Beecher's shinbone, then saw a whole flock of stars as Beecher bounced a jackrabbit jolt off the back of his neck.

Benedict wasn't given the chance to recover. With a skill born of much practice, the boys broke into a little trot over the last couple of yards and sent him rocketing out through the batwings. Stumbling to keep balance, he had no chance in the world of avoiding the big man who was coming up the steps. They came together with a crash, then in a wild confusion of arms, legs and hard language, pitched off the high gallery into the street.

It was at about the same time as Duke Benedict was doffing his expensive hat to Honey Smith in the Bird Cage Saloon that badman Dick Grid spotted the rising plume of dust from his lookout position atop Morgan's Rock. He called down to the shadows below:

'Rider comin'!'

Three dusty shapes stirred in the rock shadow – the long and gaunt Ben Sprod, the shorter one with the bowed legs, Frank Piano, and heavy-shouldered Buck Floren. The men screwed up their eyes against the yellow glare of the sun as they emerged from beneath the rocky overhang and climbed up the steep, earth-packed slope to Grid's position.

They covered less than thirty feet in all, yet by the time they had sprawled out flat on the stone behind a screen of brush beside Grid, they were sweating hard, their hard ugly faces shining under battered sombreros. It might have been cool and inviting in a place like the Bird Cage or the Shotgun down in Daybreak right now, but out here it was as hot as a kettle in hell. An hour back Frank Piano had sworn he'd seen a horned toad go by panting like a dog.

'Thar he is yonder, boss,' Dick Grid pointed, and passed Sprod the battered cavalry field-glasses.

Sprod peered through the glasses for a moment, then muttered under his breath and lowered them to work the adjustment screws to suit his eyesight.

Sprod, the outlaw they referred to in the Daybreak *Sentinel* as the Scourge of Calico Valley, looked the part. His face had sunken reptile eyes, broad cheekbones, a flat, hard nose and a vicious, slit of a mouth.

He was six-feet-two of meanness and hate and the hands which lifted the binoculars to his eyes again were long, bony and uncommonly strong. A strangler's hands.

'What do you figure, boss?' Scar-faced Floren sounded anxious after a silent minute. The horseman could be seen plainly by the naked eye now, a big man on a spotted appaloosa horse with a dog trotting in the horse's shadow. 'Is it Surprisin' Smith?'

'Mebbe,' Sprod opined in his dry, whispery voice. 'And then again, mebbe not.'

Across their leader's narrow back, Piano, Floren and Grid exchanged a look of keen disappointment. If this wasn't the pilgrim they were waiting for, then they'd wasted a whole day.

Piano made a disgusted sound in his throat and spat over the lip of the rock. 'Mebbe it's all so much hogswill anyways,' he ventured sourly. 'Mebbe them pukin' towners ain't hired a bounty-hunter to help flush us out of the valley at all. Dammit, mebbe there ain't even no ranny named Surprisin' Smith.'

'You sure are a disbelieving cuss,' said Grid, pursing meaty lips. 'I tole yuh I read all about this Smith jasper in a broadsheet. He shot and kilt Flint Brand down in Burnt River about a month back. Ain't that so, Ben?'

'Yeah, and Flint Brand was one of the best.'

'Well,' said Piano, 'I still don't believe Daybreak's gone and hired him to hunt us down, anyway.'

'I believe it,' growled Sprod. 'If I didn't I wouldn't be here fryin' my hide on this mangy rock.'

That was Frank Piano's cue to shut up and he took it. Of all the dangerous things a man could do in Calico Valley, arguing with Ben Sprod had to be about top of the list.

The oncoming horseman had covered another fifty yards. Sprod played the glasses over him slowly, growing more sharply aware that the rider wasn't the kind you were likely to meet up with just any old day along the trail.

He was one hell of a big man, with ox shoulders and a barrel of a chest. He was rigged in leather shotgun chaps, scuffed boots and a battered curl-brimmed gray Stetson tilted forward against the sun. His shirt might have been a vivid purple once but was now many shades lighter from sun and too many river-washings.

A shining object dangling from a cord around the rider's neck puzzled Sprod until he realized it was a harmonica.

The barrel chest was bared with the shirt unbuttoned to the waist and around the man's middle hung a shell belt and Colt.

Sprod's gaze lingered longest on that gunrig. The holster was of heavy, oiled leather thonged down to the muscular right thigh. The cartridge belt was also oiled and waxed against the weather, the brass tops of the shell casings glinting. The gun holster and belt in fact were the only items about the rider's person in good condition. It could easily be a gunfighter's rig, yet as Ben Sprod lowered the glasses he had his doubts.

Dick Grid began to have doubts of his own as the rider cut through the shadows flung by a gaunt, trailside finger of rock outcropping. 'Hell, Ben, he's kinda big, ain't he?' Grid's face wrinkled. 'You ever see a gunslinger that big, boss?'

'Bounty-hunters come all sizes,' snapped Sprod. But to himself he had to admit the rider looked a mite big for fast work. This pilgrim was built like a brick house and looked as if he might lift locomotives for exercise.

'Yeah, he's big right enough,' Buck Floren agreed. 'Say, mebbe his size is what's so surprisin' about him.'

Floren chuckled at his own wit but Ben Sprod was not amused. In fact Sprod was taking what Floren said seriously. There had to be some reason for tagging a man Surprising Smith.

'All right, I reckon it's him,' he said with sudden decision, bellying backwards away from the rock rim. 'C'mon, we'll get down below and make ready to take him.'

Piano, Grid and Floren wriggled backwards, then followed Sprod down beneath the overhang into the arroyo. The trio was untroubled by the possibility that the man they planned to kill might be anybody else but the man they were after. All they knew was that Daybreak was supposed to have hired a bounty-hunter to run them out of the valley, that this was the day he was scheduled to arrive, and that this big stranger was the first likely-looking loner to come up the trail all day.

If the rider was Surprising Smith, then they'd stop him cold before he got a chance to cause them any grief. If he wasn't, he'd just have to rate himself dead unlucky.

The trio exchanged confident grins as they reached their positions behind the boulders in the arroyo that cut into the black rock shadow. They checked out their guns, and waited. This was going to be almost too easy. The way that pilgrim was sitting his saddle, he looked like he'd fallen asleep.

TWO

BAD MEN OF CALICO VALLEY

Hank Brazos was not asleep, even if he looked it. He was just relaxed, content to let his appaloosa set his own pace over the last dusty miles to Daybreak while he coped with a savage hangover and the legacy of assorted kicks and blows sustained the previous night in one of the wildest brawls he'd ever been in. In the shadow of the horse, his mean looking hound, Bullpup, loped, tongue lolling. The dog was a little overhung too.

It was funny how a town could fool you, the big drifter was reflecting as he rode towards a lofty, bleached trail-side rock. On riding into Red Fork a couple of days back he'd sized it up as a one-horser about as lively as a morgue. Not his sort of town at all, considering he was a man who liked his steak thick, his whisky straight, and his fun on the violent side.

Just went to show you how appearances could lie, he thought, as he'd discovered when the lid blew off last night. A ghost of a smile touched the wide mouth as he relived the memorable scene in Frontier Street. . . .

There'd been no warning of trouble. He'd simply been escorting a certain little cowgirl out of the saloon with nothing more than a bottle and a little light courting in mind, when her pappy rode in. Pappy owned half Red Fork County. Her six big brothers were there right in back of him, and twenty dirt-mean cowboys from pappy's big spread crowding their heels. It hadn't taken the rancher long to get his message across; he didn't aim to have any daughter of his sparkin' with no flea-bitten overgrown motherless son of a saddle bum. Unquote.

Maybe pappy had sized him up about right, though Brazos was hanged if he would admit to fleas. What pappy didn't know however was that Hank Brazos, cowboy, drifter, brawler, ex-soldier and foot-loose hell-raiser, was a man who dearly loved nothing so much as a good ruckus. He was ever ready to fight, at the drop of a hat, and if nobody else was eager, he'd even drop the hat.

Brazos' smile widened, as he remembered, despite the fact that smiling pained his bruised mouth some. The fracas that had erupted then had been a classic. Pleasurably he recalled the swathe he'd cut in the cowman ranks with a handy porch bench, the heads he'd cracked, the faces he'd punched and most of all the way pappy had looked when Brazos had picked him up and tossed him through the front window of the hotel. That had been just two seconds before the sheriff had flattened him with a length of two-by-four.

The lawman had locked him up for the night, fined him ten dollars for being drunk and disorderly, and that morning had escorted him to Red Rock's town limits with the firm warning not to come back. Ever.

That was OK by Brazos, for Red Rock sure was a dreary little town, despite last night's fun. Maybe Daybreak would be a little livelier, he hoped, as he tugged out a packet of Bull Durham and twisted a brown paper quirly one-handed. If it was, then he might consider looking about for a job for, thanks to that ten-buck fine this morning, funds were running kind of low.

The thought of work depressed him a little, so to cheer himself up, he blew out a little tune on his harmonica, then sang the words of his own composition of which he was inordinately proud. The chorus ran:

'The son-of-a-bitch jumped over the fence, Goodbye my lover, goodbye.'

He thought he sounded pretty good considering last night. But Bullpup emitted a low growl and trotted ahead as if to escape the music.

'Hell, it wasn't all that danged awful,' he grinned. And then in the space of a heartbeat he wasn't grinning any more as he saw the short hair on the back of the great hound's neck bristle, its fierce yellow eyes riveted on the lofty trailside rock slanted over a narrow arroyo not much more than a hundred yards ahead.

Brazos rode on. He reached into his pocket and tugged out his Bull Durham and commenced to roll another cigarette. It was the action of a relaxed man, but from beneath his tilted hat, his eyes were stabbing at the rock and its deep shadow falling across the arroyo beneath. For a moment he saw nothing. Then the blue eyes tightened as he spotted what Bullpup had seen first; the dull glint of reflected sunlight on blue metal in those deep shadows.

Brazos let his breath run out of him in a long slow gust as he cracked a match on his thumbnail and applied it to the cigarette. His brain suddenly very clear now, he surveyed the way ahead with Bullpup growling warnings from below. If that was an ambush up ahead, then he had two choices. He could circle away down to the right and cut the trail further on, or he could find out what Mr Drygulcher used for gut-stuffing. It really wasn't all that much of a decision to make. By his book, a drygulcher rated alongside a rattler.

He sized up the situation, using an ex-soldier's know-how. Before the trail got in range of the big rock, it dipped into a dry creek bed that wound out of the timbered rocky slopes to his left. There was brush in the creek, good cover. He puffed lazily on the weed, and blue smoke wafted back across his shoulder as the trail started to curve down.

The moment he reached the bottom of the creek bed, all laziness vanished. As he rolled out of the saddle and hissed to Bullpup to stay put, crouching low, he went snaking up the creek bed, spitting out his cigarette and hauling his six-gun.

He angled through the timber that clothed the hill slope above the big rock. He ran swiftly in a crouch, and despite the fact that he weighed two hundred and twenty solid pounds, made no more noise than a stalking Apache. Hank Brazos had played these games before, and the stakes had mostly been high.

Reaching the topside of the huge rock that had helped conceal his progress from whoever waited below he heard the voices. They were tense, uncertain. Somebody cursed. Brazos stretched out on a slab of sun-whitened rock not far from the giant rock and waited. He could have been a huge lizard basking in the sun, he was so still. Sweat trickled down from his thick hair onto his face and dripped off to steam on the stone beneath him. The sun was a hammer-head on his back trying to crush him. The earth lay gasping all around.

A man appeared from out of the arroyo. He was a big scar-faced pilgrim, muscled heavily in the shoulders. He stared intently up the trail, looking for the vanished horse and rider.

A voice from the arroyo said, 'See anythin'?'

'Not a damned thing.'

'Then get up atop the rock and take a look.'

The man climbed reluctantly, now in full open view of the big still figure stretched out on the rock. Brazos could have tossed a rock and been pretty sure of nailing him, but made no move. He was waiting to see if the others would show themselves.

They didn't. The scar-faced man reached the crest of the rock and yelled down, 'I can see his hoss, Ben. Only he ain't on it!'

Curses from below. 'Somethin's gone wrong! Come on, we'll mount up and go find out!'

Brazos heard the stamp of horses in the arroyo as the man started lumbering down the rock. He couldn't wait any longer. He got to one knee.

'Hold it right there, joker!'

Scarface Floren spun, gave a startled grunt, went white and tried to use the Peacemaker .45 in his fist.

Brazos' gun beat heavy thunder, three shots clashing together in a continuous rolling roar. Floren cried out once, pitched headlong down the packed earth slope and came to rest against a small boulder staring sightlessly straight up into the yellow eye of the sun.

A small, vicious head suddenly appeared beneath the huge rock. Brazos threw himself flat, fired twice. He ducked low as answering lead came screaming back and a slug tugged his shirt. He punched fresh shells into his smoking Colt, then glimpsed the lanky, skull-faced figure leap back into the arroyo with a shout:

'He's got the drop on us! Let's git to hell and gone out of here!'

Brazos blasted a gunful of shots towards the arroyo to help them on their way. Hooves thundered, butter yellow dust climbed into the brassy sky, and then they were gone, clattering away down the arroyo bed, out of sight and out of range.

When the hoofs had drummed away to silence, Brazos rose, poked his hat back with the barrel of his gun and went down the slope to look at the dead man. He had 'drygulcher' written all over him, and right now looked the most surprised drygulcher in Calico Valley.

Cautiously, just in case, he made his way down to the arroyo and saw where they'd waited. By the look of it they'd been waiting quite a spell.

Holstering his gun, he tugged out his sack of Bull Durham and built a fresh smoke as he climbed back up to the lookout rock. His face was stony, his eyes cold as he reached the dead man and propped a dusty boot up on a stone, sucking smoke deep. The drygulcher's eyes were glazed, his life's blood very red against the sun-whitened stone.

The big man's mouth turned bitter as he stooped and heaved the corpse over his shoulder as if it weighed nothing. As he trod heavily back to his horse, he felt the fire of battle burn away inside him, to be replaced by simple anger. What in hell kind of place was this anyway when an almost-law-abiding citizen could come within a touch of getting drygulched in broad daylight almost in sight of a town?

A damned good question, he figured, and one he meant to get an answer to, just as soon as he reached Daybreak.

Daybreak came out of its late afternoon lethargy with a bang, and the bang came from one hundred and eighty pounds of dead man landing on the front porch of the law-office.

Deputy Sam Fink was asleep in his chair when the jail-house shook end to end, and by the time he knuckled his eyes, got to his feet, put on his hat and limped out, they were converging on the jailhouse from all over.

Sam Fink and the citizens of Daybreak immediately found themselves in a dilemma. They didn't know which commanded more attention, the dusty dead man who had been so unceremoniously dumped on the boards, or the big, purple-shirted stranger who sat his saddle looking like a month of stormy weather.

'Drygulcher,' the big rider snapped. 'Jumped me comin' in up by that big rock on the east trail. It's a hell of a note when a man's got to shoot his way into a town.'

Sam Fink blinked, then collected himself and came out onto the gallery and turned the dead man over.

'Jumped up Judas!' exclaimed the deputy. 'It's Buck Floren!'

Uproar.

With barely concealed impatience, Brazos waited for them to calm down some, then demanded, 'Who's Buck Floren?'

They all spoke at once, but he managed to get the drift that Buck Floren was a member of Ben Sprod's bunch and that Ben Sprod was known around as the Scourge of Calico Valley.

'Yeah, well, that's mighty interestin' I'm sure, but why the blazes was this joker and his pards gunnin' for me?'

Nobody could even guess. There was a lot of excited babble, and then a fat man with a beard growing almost to his middle said, 'You git a sight of the others, mister?'

Brazos nodded. 'One of 'em. Ugly varmint with a little head, kinda like a snake.'

'Ben Sprod!'

A dozen voices said the name in unison. Then a big man with a big voice said, 'By Taos, boys, this here's a stroke of luck. Ben showin' up right on our doorstep when we're fixin' to take after him. C'mon, let's go tell the mayor.'

'Carbrook's outa town,' another yelled. 'I seen him ridin' out to his ranch an hour back.'

'Then go fetch him, Josh,' the fat man shouted excitedly. 'Time's a-wastin'. Boys, go git your hosses and rifles. We'll ride out as soon as Carbrook gets back.'

Brazos nodded in satisfaction then swung his horse away and forced it through the crowd. If they aimed to get a posse out after the badmen who'd jumped him, then that was all that concerned him for the moment. Right now he needed a drink, lordy did he need one.

Cutting across the street to the first building he saw with batwing doors, he swung down and went up the steps, thinking only about that drink.

Then very suddenly he had something else to think about as the batwings burst open and a dude came hurtling out to cannon into him with violent force. In a confusion of arms, legs and curses, both rolled off the gallery to land in the street sending up a great cloud of dust and frightening the hell out of the racked horses.

It took Brazos a full ten seconds to extricate himself from the tangle and lurch to his feet, and by that time his temper was alight again. This, he gritted through clenched teeth, was the last straw. Somebody was going to get his lumps, and who deserved them more than this runaway tinhorn?

The big, knuckle-scarred fist was cocked to let fly as the angry-faced gambler staggered to his feet in the dust, swearing like a muleskinner in a fine Eastern accent. The bomb was on its way when something about that voice clicked in Brazos' brain. The fist stopped. He stared at the face before him through the clearing dust and his jaw fell open with disbelief.

'The Yank!'

'Well, I'll be a dirty name,' came the equally astonished response. 'The Johnny Reb!'

Violence fled from two faces to be replaced by disbelieving grins. Two hands gripped, hands that had only met once before, and that on a day of madness, war and death, a day conjured up immediately now for two men who'd met one historic day in Georgia, and parted never dreaming they might one day meet again.

'Well, I'm busted!' Hank Brazos said finally. 'The last joker I ever expected to bump into. What in hell are you doin' out here, Yank?' And then, before the other could answer, 'Dammit, but it just hit me. I don't even know your handle.'

'Duke Benedict, Reb,' the handsome gambler smiled. 'And you?'

'Brazos, Hank Brazos.' He flung his big arms wide in an expansive gesture. 'Well, Judas, man, this calls for a drink, don't it?'

'I should smile it does, Brazos,' Benedict replied readily. He swung towards the batwings of the Bird Cage, then halted with a frown at the recollection of a certain mean-faced bounty-hunter and an irate saloonkeeper. 'Maybe you'll find the Shotgun Saloon more to your liking, Reb. Confidentially, the liquor in here isn't up to much.'

'Still got that there fancy accent, huh?' big Brazos grinned as they strode in the direction of the Shotgun Saloon. 'You know, that's one thing I always remembered about that there day . . . that foreign damn accent of your'n.'

'That accent as you call it,' Benedict replied amiably, 'cost my folks about a thousand dollars to get for me at college. And talking about remembering things, it seems I recall that day that I'd never met a man who seemed to enjoy fighting as much as you. Judging by the look of your face, Reb, I'd say you were still enjoying yourself.' Brazos ruefully rubbed the marks of recent violence on his craggy, sun-bronzed young face as they shouldered through the swinging doors of the Shotgun Saloon.

'Just a run-in with a passel of cowpokes at Red Fork,' he explained. Then, nonchalantly jerking a thumb at his bullet-burned shoulder, 'And this here little memento I picked up just outa town. Drygulched. But all that ain't important, Yank. Name your poison.'

'Bourbon's been poisoning me for years.'

'A bottle of bourbon!' Brazos bellowed, slamming a fist down on the tinny bar of the Shotgun and sending myopic little barman Charlie Bird scuttling for the shelves. 'A bottle of bourbon for Hank Brazos and his old pard Duke Benedict!'

Old pards? No, they'd never been that, and likely never could be, this footloose young Texan with the barn-door shoulders and the handsome, expensively educated Easterner with the Yankee accent and the gambler's eyes. Yet as they repaired to a table and lifted glasses, each in his own way was conscious of the bond between them that was perhaps even stronger than friendship, maybe even stronger than blood. For what could be stronger than a tie born in the savage heat of battle, forged in blood, hammered by the cannon's steel and tempered in the blood of comrades? No, what bound them was stronger than friendship; they were bound forever by memory of the dead. . . .

'Well, what do we drink to, Yank?'

Duke Benedict's face grew grave. 'Why, I guess we should drink to Pea Ridge, Reb.'

'Pea Ridge,' Brazos replied, lifting his glass and the name sent memory swirling back.

Pea Ridge. . .

THREE

ANGRY GROW THE GUNS

The rooster crowed as if this morning were just like any other and flapped its wings against the smoky gray sky of dawn.

The tent tops of John Leo Brett's 6th Texas Brigade were dimly outlined by the gray eastern smudge. It revealed the thirty silent mounted men in the butternut gray of the Confederacy and the small, four-wheeled wagon.

Again the rooster crowed. In the command tent, a solitary lamp burned.

John Leo Brett's face was the same tired gray as his uniform as he stared across his desk at Lieutenant Tom Flint and Sergeant Brazos. The South was in its death agonies, the glorious dream a nightmare. Its defeat was written there, in the haggard, once handsome face of a man of thirty-five who looked closer to sixty.

'Any last questions?'

The small lieutenant and the wide-shouldered young sergeant shook their heads. They'd gone over the plan of action already a dozen times with Brett during the long sleepless night just past. They were to leave at first light with the wagon and make their way down the two-mile length of Channing Valley. The brigade's artillery would cover their progress the length of the valley to Pea Ridge, which may or may not be in the hands of the Federals. They were to cross Pea Ridge and then drive west from bloody Georgia; west across the Mississippi, southwest across the vast uncertainty of Texas, south across the Rio Grande into Mexico, where the Southern General Nathan Forrest had repaired to set up the Second Confederacy which would rise to take the place of the beaten and glorious First.

Into Forrest's hands they were to deliver the contents of the wagon: two hundred thousand dollars in gold pieces, the final wealth of the South. If they failed, the South would never rise again.

No, there were no questions.

A salute, a handshake, then out into the chill gray morning. The detail moved off. The rooster crowed a third time, its piercing cry carrying far in the hushed morning, all the way across the shell-torn hills to the blue ranks of the enemy – where Captain Duke Benedict of the 10th Vermont Militia shaved with the aid of a small mirror propped against a scarred tree trunk and a flickering stub of candle.

The stubble-jawed soldiers squatting about in the

gloom watched the officer with puzzled, admiring eyes. Most of them were too wearied by battle even to wash, yet there was the captain, shaving his good-looking pan exactly the way he had every morning as far back as any of them could remember. There was no doubt about it, the captain was one hell of a dandy, but by God he was a soldier to follow, and those fifty who were riding with him that historic week in Georgia were ready to ride with him to the gates of hell if need be.

Benedict finished his toilet, buttoned up his dark blue jacket and snuffed out the candle. He took out his service pistol, and was checking it when Lieutenant Miller spoke.

'Where to today, Captain?'

Benedict put the revolver away, looked west. 'Pea Ridge,' he said. 'It seems there might be a nest of Johnny Reb snipers over there. We're to clean it out.'

Pea Ridge. The listening men turned the name over in their minds. It sounded like an easy detail. About time they drew one.

Had there been no fog they would never have made it, for with the Union artillery in command of the northern ridges of Channing Valley, and their own guns snarling from the south, the valley was a no-man's land, a place of death and horror. But they'd gambled on the fog and it was there today as it had been every morning, perhaps a little thicker from the hellish smoke that drifted down from the ridges where the cannons stormed.

Riding at the head of the detail at the side of Lieutenant Flint, Hank Brazos found it almost impossible to think in the shuddering thunder of the guns. All he knew was that they'd ridden three quarters the length of the valley without losing a man, and that Pea Ridge could be only a few hundred yards ahead. Soon they would be able to see it rising out of the fog.

Upon reaching the ridge, they would have to leave the safety of the fog screen and rush up the naked, shell-pocked slopes in full sight of the Union guns. That slope would likely be the most dangerous strip of trail between Georgia and Mexico: if they made that, they believed they could make it all the way.

The horsemen ducked instinctively as a shell whistled low. The noise of the barrage was increasing. Looking up towards the ridges they could see the Union positions wrapped in seething gunsmoke which glowed with dust-red patches. The red patches spread out, devoured the smoke and curtained the sky and made a deep cliff face of red as the attack intensified. The Confederate batteries retaliated and the whole valley shook.

Minutes later they emerged from the fog and went up the slopes of Pea Ridge at a run. Immediately the Union guns lowered their aim. Around them the earth began to erupt.

A soldier in a Confederate battery position fifty yards to the left of the column stuck his head out from the earth and gave them a shout of encouragement as they passed, slashing whips at the wagon horses. Almost in the same instant, the battery position was hit, blown into the air like a bursting triangle, and the dark fragments were pieces of guns and metal and bodies of the crew. Another shell struck and the column was hit. Another. Slabs of timber falling to the earth. Pieces of a bunker roof. A horse tumbling from the sky. The broken body of a man blown into the air, fell down and was immediately torn into the air again by a second blast.

Then they were in the trees. The shells continued to search, but without accuracy. They were safe.

They hauled up briefly atop the ridge to spell the horses for a moment and take stock. They'd lost seven men with two wounded. Not good, but it could have been much worse. The sergeant and the lieutenant exchanged a silent glance. They were going to make it.

They moved on and the sounds of the guns were dimming behind them, when, incredibly, from higher up the slopes of Pea Ridge, came the thin, tinny and unforgettable sound of a trumpet signaling attack.

They swept down from a line of magnolias, a line of shouting, blue-clad soldiers led by a handsome officer with an upraised saber that reflected the crimson light of the morning.

'Hurrah!' they shouted. 'Hurrah! Hurrah! Hurrah!'

There was no time to retreat, no time to run, no time for anything but fight. The guns exploded from the ranks of blue and answered back from the gray. A speeding Federal cavalryman went down with a jagged scream that seemed to hang in the air. Trooper Billy-Joe Ashbrook of South Carolina fell and died without a sound, gone in a moment after almost four years of war. The ragged fire stuttered out, smoke rose thick; blue and gray figures fell.

Then they came together in a storm of screams and shots and the bite of cold steel. Sergeant Hank Brazos became oblivious of anybody but those who wore blue. The smoke was choking thick now. He shot a man in the face at five feet, then another, yet another. A Yankee rushed past him with a long rifle and a gleaming bayonet. Brazos whirled. Too late. The bayonet pierced the heart of Lieutenant Tom Flint who'd just got to his feet after being unhorsed.

The soldier reefed the dripping bayonet free and his face, an ugly mask of triumph, swung at Brazos. Brazos triggered and the hammer only clicked. The big Yankee snarled and rushed. Brazos side-stepped, grabbed the rifle. The Yankee fought him. He was a strong man, but the Confederate sergeant was doubly strong. He reefed the gun away and ripped the man apart with his own blade. He swung and threw it at another rushing figure. The spearing weapon thudded into the man's chest and he fell. Brazos snatched up a fallen gun and he was firing again.

Time swept by. Now they were driving the Yankees back up the slope, then it was they who were being driven.

The 6th Texas Brigade broke, reformed, broke again. They took cover and for hours the guns held sway. They grew impatient, the attacks began again with sabers, bayonets, fists and boots and stones. There was a madness in the conflict that wouldn't let either faction retreat or surrender. They were evenly matched in numbers and hatred. Men died, horses fell, the hours dragged on. The sounds from the valley dimmed, the main impact of the battle was passing them by, yet still they raged on, the tattered gray remnants led by a youthful giant of a sergeant, the Federals inspired again and again by the handsome captain they'd followed for so long, and now seemed destined to follow all the way to the grave.

*

It was mid-afternoon. Hank Brazos lay in a shell crater with two companions. Three men alive out of thirty-two.

Ninety feet up the slope, the overturned wagon lay, the heavy steel plated trunk containing the gold upturned in a ditch. Another sixty feet beyond that, behind a fallen tree, the remnants of the Union force sniped down at their position. There were four men behind that tree with Captain Duke Benedict; five men left of fifty. The factions had cut one another to shreds and now it seemed they would go on fighting until nobody was left. That was war. They didn't question it. They were men who'd long since ceased to question this madness. . . .

And kill themselves to the last man they certainly would have, but for what happened an hour later. Another charge from the same line of magnolias, but no trumpet blew this time, no blue uniforms in the sun. Nor any gray. For the horde of horsemen that came charging down with blazing guns, hurdling the dead and dying, and shouting a fierce battle cry that had nothing to do with North or South, were not soldiers. They were bearded, wild-eyed men in buckskin and even before the chant of, 'Rangle! Rangle!' washed down over the stunned and battle-numbed survivors below, both Federals and Rebels had guessed who they were.

Rangle's Raiders! A rag-tail band of marauding privateers who fought for neither North nor South but who preyed upon both, the offal and scum sweepings of a dozen borders banded together to rape and plunder under the leadership of a man whose name had become a stench in the nostrils of every fighting man, whether he be Union or Confederate: Bo Rangle, one time outlaw and killer, now leader of the most despised band of hellions on either side of the Mississippi.

The Union handful took the first full brunt of the Raiders' charge and though having already fought themselves to a standstill, they fought on bravely again, aided by the guns of Hank Brazos and his two men. A dozen marauders fell in that first brutal clash and there was astonishment in Rangle's ranks at the fierceness of the resistance. Yet defeat was inevitable and finally, with his last man dead, Captain Duke Benedict was driven from cover. A gun in each hand, he came backing down past the overturned gold wagon, blasting back at the enemy every step. In the shell crater at Brazos' elbow, a man swung his rifle at the blue-clad figure, but Brazos knocked it down.

'You don't back shoot a brave soldier!' he snapped. Then cupping his hands to his mouth, he roared. 'Hey, Yank. Git on down here!'

Benedict turned his head in astonishment. As he did, Brazos showed his head and shoulders, and with a gun in each hand, sent snarling lead screaming past him to cut down a pair of charging renegades. That was enough for Benedict. Punching off two more shots, he ducked low and dashed for the crater, covering the last ten feet in a long, diving leap. Landing inside the crater, he rolled on his shoulders and came to his feet, still with his six-guns in hand.

'Thanks, Reb,' was all he said – was all he had time to say as Bo Rangle led his men towards the crater in what was meant to be a final charge.

But it didn't turn out that way. The marauder charge ran into a vicious scythe of fire that blasted six more men into eternity and cut down more than that number of horses. Amazed, Rangle withdrew to regroup, then after a minute, charged again.

This time they almost made it, getting to within twenty feet of the crater, but again the fire of Brazos and Benedict broke the attack and drove them back.

By now, Brazos' and Benedict's were the only guns that spoke from the crater, for Brazos' last two men lay sprawled dead in the yellow mud, brave to the last.

Twice more in the next ten minutes the raiders attacked and twice more were driven off with heavy loss of life. Dusk was settling as the two hollow-eyed defenders wearily reloaded their smoking weapons and watched the raiders grouping yet again in the trees. Brazos had dragged a box of ammunition into the shell hole with him when they'd taken refuge there, but it was almost empty. Another attack would exhaust it; another attack would be the last.

That last attack never came. Ten minutes dragged by, another ten. Darkness crept over the land. A long way off now, the cannons muttered. Somewhere up the slopes a dying man called for his mother and a chill wind rose to rustle the trees and carry away the last of the gunsmoke.

Then the darkness fell like a club. Stealthy footsteps sounded up the slope, drawing nearer. The men in the shell crater exchanged a glance, their faces dim ovals in the blackness.

'Looks like they're movin' in to finish us off, Yank.'

'Seems like it, Reb.' A short pregnant silence, then: 'We won't see sun-up.'

'Reckon not.'

'Would you do something for me, Reb?'

'What's that?'

'Shake hands. If I've got to die, I'd as soon do it in the company of the best fighter I ever met . . . even if he is a Johnny Reb.'

Their hands clasped in the gloom. 'That goes for me too, Yank,' Hank Brazos said softly, then stiffened and turned at a sound close by.

'What are you doing?' Benedict whispered, peering intently uphill. 'You see anything, Reb?'

Brazos couldn't . . . but suddenly he didn't have to. That heavy dragging sound identified itself.

'The box!' he gasped. 'They're takin' the box!' He cursed. 'Goddamn it, they must have known about it right along.'

'Known about what?' Benedict asked.

Brazos didn't reply. Instead, he cut loose with his six-gun. Immediately a storm of shots came back from the darkness, shots that tore and raked at the earth and drove them down to hug the bottom of the crater.

His face pressed into the mud, Brazos was conscious of a great bitterness as the lead continued to storm. He realized now that the raider attack was no accident. Bo Rangle had got wind of the shipment and had come hunting it. Jumped-up Judas, he'd rather let the goddamn Yankees have it than a rat like Rangle!

It was a long time before the shooting finally stopped.

They heard the raiders drifting away, and far away in

the distance, the dim sound of a wagon wheel striking a rock. Yet they couldn't be sure that all the enemy had gone, and were forced to keep to the crater until dawn. Only then, with the sickly yellow light spilling down the bloody slopes of Pea Ridge, did they realize they were safe. Bo Rangle was gone. All that was left was the dead.

They came out of the crater together, walked silently among the littered bodies. Pea Ridge was incredibly silent after the insanity of sound that unforgettable day. Blue uniforms lay side by side with gray. The faces of young and old stared up into the dim light.

The battle of Pea Ridge was over.

They stopped finally together beside the overturned wagon. Their eyes met and locked for a long silent moment. Then almost as if by a prearranged signal, each man lifted his right hand. The hands met and clasped for a long moment.

'So long, Yank.'

'Goodbye, Reb.'

That was all, a handshake, a simple farewell. Yet as both men trudged slowly away from that place of death, to go their separate ways, each was aware that for as long as they lived, neither of them would forget the other and that crimson day in history they'd shared on the bloody slopes of Pea Ridge, Georgia.

And so they parted, forever they'd thought, until Fate decreed otherwise, six months and many hundreds of miles later, in a dusty cowtown in Kansas.

FOUR

CONFEDERATE GOLD

The barkeep, Charlie Bird, brought two fresh whiskies across to the table and picked up the empty bottle. It had been some reunion party.

The barkeep beamed at the best customers he'd had in months. 'And another beer for the dog, Mr Brazos?'

Brazos frowned down at Bullpup trying to figure out how many beers they'd already poured into the tin dish on the floor. He couldn't recall, so he snapped his fingers to make the dog sit up. Bullpup grunted and assumed a sitting position which was marred by a thirty degree list to starboard.

'No more for him,' Brazos decided firmly. 'He's had enough.'

Charlie Bird shuffled off to the bar, shaking his head, wonderingly. It was a long time since he'd witnessed such impressive consumption of liquor by man or beast. And though both his clients were now showing inevitable signs of what they'd taken aboard, it seemed that they still weren't ready to quit.

Charlie Bird and the dozen seedy denizens of the Shotgun could have been forgiven for getting the idea that Hank Brazos and Duke Benedict were just a couple of drunks, but that was not the case. Certainly both men were stern drinkers, yet it was the uniqueness of the situation, the unexpectedness of their reunion, which seemed to demand something large and liquid in the way of celebration.

Heedless of the interest they aroused among Charlie Bird and his customers, Benedict and Brazos went on reminiscing and soon Bird came back with more drinks.

This time, the glowering Bullpup, incensed at not getting his tin dish refilled, took a short-tempered snap at the barkeep's heels.

'That's some dog you've got there, Reb,' Benedict observed as Charlie Bird demonstrated a remarkable agility in reaching the sanctuary of his bar.

'Sure is,' Brazos agreed proudly and the dog seemed to puff up, as if aware that they were talking about him.

The hound which Hank Brazos had managed to keep with him during the two years he'd served in the Army and in his months of drifting ever since Appomattox, was nothing if not eye catching. Part bulldog, part wolf and part heaven alone knew what, it weighed well over a hundred pounds with a head like a buffalo's. It was a dirty brown color with a few white splotches, one blue eye, one brown and a mouth big enough to let in full grown cats.

It sat on its haunches now at Brazos' side wearing a look of self-satisfaction after taking a taste of Charlie Bird. Its pink mouth was wide open as it panted in the heat. Occasionally it licked its lips with a big red tongue, smacking on the taste of the beer.

'Almost seems human when he looks you in the eye,' Benedict observed, taking a slender Havana from his expensive gold cigar case.

'Oh, he's smart enough when he wants to be,' Brazos conceded, and nudged the great head affectionately with the toe of his boot as he recalled how Bullpup's sharpness had saved his bacon that afternoon. Then, lifting his beer, he frowned thoughtfully. 'Speakin' of dogs, Yank, you ever crossed trails with Bo Rangle since you got out of the Army?'

Duke Benedict's face sharpened at the question. Suspicion leapt immediately into his eyes. 'What makes you ask that?'

Seeing the sudden change of mood, Brazos lowered his glass and frowned in puzzlement.

'I say somethin' wrong, Yank?'

Duke Benedict studied the rugged brown face across the table for a moment, then felt that brief stab of suspicion begin to fade. No, he reassured himself, Big Brazos couldn't have any idea of why he was here. Brains obviously weren't his specialty. He'd had ample chance to get to know the man now. Back at Pea Ridge, Georgia, seemingly an eternity ago now, all he'd known about this big Reb sergeant, was that he was the best fighting man he'd ever come across. During the hours of their reunion here in the Shotgun, however, he'd come to realize that but for what had happened, this big drifter was about the last person he'd ever sit down to share a convivial drink with. Hank Brazos was rough, illiterate, uncouth, not a Benedict man by any means. But harmless enough, Benedict decided, touching a match to the end of his cigar and putting on the friendly smile once again.

'Why, Rangle's still around,' he said easily in answer to the question. 'He turned outlaw like a lot of those marauders after the War. He's wanted all over by the law.'

Brazos nodded thoughtfully. 'Sure would like to meet up with that there varmint one bright sunny day you know, Benedict.'

'Wouldn't mind it myself, I guess.'

Brazos took another sip of his drink. 'You know what was in that there box we lost up there that day on Pea Ridge, do you?'

Benedict nodded, and a hard cold glint came into his eyes.

'Yes . . . two hundred thousand dollars in Confederate gold.'

Brazos grinned. 'We figgered you were after it.'

'Didn't know a thing about it. We were out looking for trouble that day, we sighted you and seeing we outnumbered you we attacked.'

Benedict puffed a reflective cloud of blue smoke at the overhead light. 'Two hundred thousand!' he said softly and shook his head. 'I'll allow when I heard about it later I was set back some. I guess if I'd known about that gold that day I'd have fought even harder.'

'You'd have been goin' some to do that, but I reckon I know how you felt. Two hundred thousand iron men ain't somethin' you come across every day. I'd reckon at that time the North could've put that gold to mighty good use.'

Benedict cocked an elegant eyebrow, and the clipped Eastern accent was just a little slurred. 'The North?' A cold smile. 'Why certainly I suppose they could have put it to good use – if I'd been fool enough to turn it over.'

'You mean you wouldn't have?'

'Do I look a fool?'

'You'd have kept the gold for yourself?'

'Two hundred grand? I should smile I would have. Who wouldn't have?'

'Well . . . me for one, Yank.'

Benedict made a gesture of disbelief. 'Hogswill, Reb, I can't swallow that. Say our positions had been reversed that day and it was you who came across a fortune in Federal gold. You mean to say you'd have turned it over to Jeff Davis? Like hell you would.'

'Sure I would. I ain't no thief.'

For the second time in five minutes, Duke Benedict's eyes stabbed suspiciously at his companion. The professional gambler could read a man's face like he could read a deck of cards. He searched for signs that Brazos was putting him on, but saw nothing but truth in Hank Brazos' rugged young face, found only honesty in the guileless blue eyes that looked back levelly at him from beneath the unruly thatch of straw-colored hair.

Duke Benedict felt irritation begin to rise within him. The polished adventurer with the worldly cynicism forged by years of gambling, gunfighting, soldiering and looking out for Number One, could never figure an honest man. To be dumb and illiterate was bad enough, but to be honest to boot was just too many marks against a man regardless of Pea Ridge or anything else.

Brazos sensed the beginning of a rift, but before it could be widened any further, they were interrupted by the arrival of Mayor Carbrook and Deputy Sam Fink.

The mayor, who had just been brought back to town from his little part-time spread out beyond the river, was looking for Brazos and lost no time in getting straight down to business. He'd already heard all about the shoot-out at Morgan's Rock and had inspected Floren's remains on the way to the saloon. Now he wanted a first-hand account from Brazos himself.

Brazos obliged laconically and mellowed somewhat by booze he made the clash sound more like a casual rough-house than the deadly clash it had been.

The mayor heard him out, then explained the position in Daybreak. The Town Council of Daybreak had hired a bounty-hunter named Surprising Smith to assist in running out the notorious Ben Sprod who had been plaguing the valley for too long. Now they knew Sprod's bunch was close about, the town had got up a posse. Would the two gents care to join?

The offer was declined without thanks. Brazos had already seen more than enough of Ben Sprod, he explained, around a couple of impressive whisky-belches, and Benedict assured Mr Mayor that tempting as the prospect of good healthy exercise in the open air undoubtedly was, he'd rather stay around Johnny Street and whistle at girls when the wind was blowing petticoats around.

Some of Benedict's affability had been restored by the time the two men tromped out, looking disappointed. Signaling for another round, he said, 'This town's got plenty problems you know, Reb. And not just Sprod, either.'

'How come, Yank?'

Duke Benedict smiled. The situation he'd discovered in Daybreak was just the sort calculated to touch his funny-bone.

Leaning forward he said, 'Did you happen to notice that big new brick building two blocks down the main stem on your way into town today, Reb?'

'Why yeah, matter of fact I did. Struck me as kinda curious now I recall. Didn't look like no bank or hotel or saloon like I ever seen. What is it?'

'Daybreak's brand new bordello.'

'Well I'll be dogged,' Brazos chuckled appreciatively. 'They sure do things in a big way hereabouts. But where's the problems come in, Benedict?'

'Well, as you might guess, there are people around town who aren't exactly tickled at having the biggest sporting house in two hundred miles thrown up on their main stem. As a matter of fact there's talk of a real ruckus breaking out tomorrow night when Belle Shilleen opens the new house for business. A bunch of worthy ladies known as the Christian Ladies of Daybreak have sworn to stop the opening, matter of fact.'

'A ruckus you say? Don't sound like much of a ruckus twixt a bunch of fat ladies and a passel of sportin' gals.'

'I'm not so sure. There's bad blood between Belle and some of the town, while the CLOD ladies have been busy drumming up support to try to stop the opening. Belle seems to think they really mean business.'

'Belle? You sound like you know this little lady personal, Yank.'

'And why not? Say, you're not pure as well as honest, are you?'

'Pure as whitewashed snow,' Brazos grinned. Then, 'But who needs whorehouses?'

'A good whorehouse can be a home away from home – wonder who said that? Anyway, that's no never-mind, Reb. What say we treat ourselves to a change of scenery?'

'Hey, hold hard a minute. You ain't proposin' we go—'

'No, not Belle's,' Benedict anticipated with a laugh, getting up. One slight stagger and then he was steady on his feet. 'I mean to the Bird Cage. This place is beginning to bore me.'

'Suits me,' Brazos said readily. He came erect and followed Benedict to the doors with Bullpup lurching alcoholically at his heels. 'But I thought you said the liquor was poor up there.'

'There are other attractions in the world besides whisky.'

'Like what?'

'Like a certain little lady,' Benedict confided, pushing out through the doors. 'Just met her today, Reb, and she's really something. You'll like her. Honey Smith is her name.' His grin faded a notch as he added, '*Mrs* Honey Smith.'

'Widow woman, huh?'

'Not so you'd notice. No, she's got a husband right enough – Mr Surprising Smith – who right now should be off with the posse after Sprod's bunch. I hope.'

'The bounty-hunter Carbrook spoke about?' Brazos grinned admiringly. 'Say, you just don't give a damn, do you, Yank?'

'Not a blue-eyed damn.'

'Tell me, what's so surprisin' about this varmint anyway?'

Benedict concentrated on that as they picked their way down the rickety steps.

'Well, Honey declares he picked up that handle by surprising so many badmen on the dodge, just when they thought they were in the clear. But me, I entertain the belief that the surprising thing about him, is that such an ugly, mean-eyed little rooster could have landed himself such a good-looking wife.'

They laughed together at that and moved along the street. The fresh air was hardly sobering and they needed a fair width of street as they walked.

It had turned chilly since sundown and some quality in the air did not hold the dust, so that the air was crystal clear in Johnny Street. A big bunch of men had gathered out in front of the jailhouse, leaning against the buildings or perched up on the hitch rail where a number of horses were tied. The posse hadn't left yet after all. They looked like they weren't in a hurry. Conversation faded as Benedict and the big drifter who'd gunned Buck Floren went by with the great dog swaggering along behind.

'I'll back Sprod,' was Brazos' comment after he'd had a good look at them.

'No takers,' grinned Benedict as they mounted the gallery of the Bird Cage Saloon and walked through the heavy slabs of yellow lamplight slanting through the windows. A split second later both were diving low and clawing for their six-guns, as without a hint of warning, the Bird Cage shuddered to its foundations with a crashing storm of gunfire from the other side of the batwing doors.

FIVE

ALLIES AGAIN

Together, they lifted cautious heads. No hot lead came snarling from the saloon. They got to their feet, six-guns glinting in the yellow light splashing from the windows. Nothing happened. No shouts of alarm, no more shots.

They went to the batwings, looked in. No scene of blood and chaos greeted their eyes. Instead, they saw a group of drinkers interestedly examining a playing card nailed to a wall beam. The playing card was shot full of holes, and across the room, refilling a smoking gun and smirking with self-satisfaction under the admiring gaze of the crowd and his bright-eyed wife, stood Surprising Smith. The bounty-hunter had generously agreed to give the locals a little exhibition of his gun skill while they waited on Mayor Carbrook, and in so doing had just about scared the pants off two innocent passers-by.

Brazos swore, motioned to Bullpup to stay put and pushed into the room. Benedict followed the broad back through the batwings, even more peeved than Brazos. And the sight of pretty little Honey Smith batting her admiring eyelashes up at her mean-faced little pipsqueak gunman husband didn't improve his mood at all. Well if they wanted to see. Shooting. . . .

'Step aside!' he yelled suddenly to the group around the upright, and barely giving them time to get clear, grabbed out both white-handled guns and cut loose.

It all happened so quickly that half the saloon was taken by surprise. With the guns sounding like cannons, men dived for cover, girls shrieked, and Hank Brazos hunched his shoulders and pulled his battered hat defensively down around his ears.

It was well for those in the vicinity of the upright that they ducked for cover, for though five bullets chopped the card, the bourbon exacted its heavy toll and the other seven bullets found various targets including two bottles, the piano. Flash Jimmy Chadwick's hard-hitter hat, and Harp Moody's pet pussy cat.

A shocked silence engulfed the room. Duke Benedict shook his head critically. 'Drawing a little to the left,' he decided finally with the air of the true professional. 'I'll have to watch that.'

A fractured wire in the piano twanged and the saloon came to life. White-faced men rose from the floor plastered in sawdust and cigarette butts. Flash Jimmy Chadwick poked a finger through a neat round hole in his hard-hitter and rolled his eyes heavenward, lips moving in a silent prayer of gratitude. A considerate customer draped a canvas faro table cover over what was left of Moody's cat, while Moody himself advanced ominously up the bar-room towards Kansas' answer to Wild Bill Hickok.

With heavy tread, bouncers Beecher and Quade followed, while up on his high perch, Joe Crook cocked both hammers of his scattergun.

His eyes focused on Benedict, who was giving Honey Smith his best profile as he went about reloading his guns, Moody counted all the way up to ten, then put on a phony admiring smile.

'Benedict, that sure was some shootin'.'

Benedict beamed. He was even drunker than Brazos, who was having a little trouble holding himself up against the bar and announcing proudly if somewhat inaccurately to a couple of shaken barflies, that 'old' Duke Benedict was his very own personal old Army buddy.

'I'm a shooting fool,' Benedict confided proudly. 'You certainly are,' Moody agreed right from the heart. 'Say, mind if I take a look at those guns of yours? I'd admire to see 'em close.'

'You're close enough,' Benedict smiled, and was about to holster when Joe Crook rasped:

'Give!'

For the second time that day, Benedict found himself staring up at those two big barrels. He sighed.

'Now take it easy, Moody '

'Give!' It was Moody's turn to snap. Benedict sighed again, then reluctantly passed his guns across.

Harp Moody stepped back two paces, thrust the Colts in his belt and growled:

'All right, boys, throw the bum out. And this time, really throw him.'

Benedict yelled a protest at Moody's order, then cursed as two steely pairs of hands took hold of his person and turned him violently towards the door.

'Hey, just a blue-eyed minute!' bellowed Brazos, lurching forward. 'Get your hands off my old buddy, you jaspers!'

Beecher obeyed promptly, but only to have his hands free to belt the big drifter on the point of the jaw. Brazos grinned happily and retaliated with a smashing right cross that lifted the burly Beecher a clear six inches off the sawdust and sent him rocketing back into Quade and Benedict, all three going down in a chaotic heap of arms, legs and broken furniture.

Delighted with the results of his handiwork, Brazos spat on his palms, rubbed them together briskly and challenged the entire room.

'Step right up, boys! One at a time or all at once, it makes no never-mind to me!'

There had been times, quite a few times in fact when Hank Brazos had issued a challenge such as that and found no takers. There had been saloons full of hardcases in other towns who'd taken one look at those shoulders, the great fists and the eager expression on the broad, battle-scarred young face and decided to stick to drinking.

This was not one of those times. The presence of Surprising Smith and the awareness that Benedict and his sidekick were drunk, put boldness into faint hearts. They came at Brazos in a rush.

A mite surprised, Brazos managed to shake loose four of Burk Spanger's teeth and balloon the ear of another before being bowled over by sheer weight of numbers. Somehow he fought his way back to his feet. The room was whirling about him, a sea of faces, bobbing lights, and he suddenly realized Benedict was beside him. Shoulder to shoulder they waded in, and for one wild moment it looked as though they were holding back the tide. Then Benedict went down and out, and Brazos reeled as a bottle caromed off his hard head.

Mick Quade was quick to take advantage as Brazos staggered back on rubbery knees, and knocked him as cold as a Colorado Christmas with a forty-pound hardwood chair.

The saloon was still rocking to the thump of Brazos' two hundred and twenty pounds hitting the floorboards, when Mayor Humphrey Carbrook and Deputy Sam Fink came barging in through the batwings, followed by the posse men.

Mayor Carbrook took one disgusted look about and didn't hesitate. Daybreak had more than enough troubles of its own at the moment without drunken gamblers and brawling drifters making things worse.

'Lock them up!' he instructed Deputy Fink. Waiting only as long as it took eight strong men to stagger out the doors under the combined weight of the unconscious trouble-makers, he then collected his posse men together, and with Surprising Smith at his side, stamped out and crossed the street to where the horses were waiting.

The way things were going, the mayor huffed to himself as he mounted up and led the posse out, it looked like being a damned sight more peaceable out hunting Ben Sprod than here in town.

*

The girls of Belle Shilleen's were glum as they watched the posse men lope past below their balcony, then take the trail out of town.

'Drat!' pouted Kitty Kellick. 'They *did* go! I thought it was all just big talk.'

'So did I,' lamented leggy Gypsy Jones. 'Golly, they mightn't be back for the openin' Friday night.'

'Won't be like a real opening without all the boys,' chimed in Sweet Shirley. And amongst the 'boys' she was referring to, were some of the leading citizens of Daybreak.

'All right, girls,' an authoritative voice spoke from the open doorway behind them. 'No time for slacking. There won't *be* any opening tomorrow night unless we get everything ready in time.'

The girls sighed, but turned obediently away from the balcony.

Belle Shilleen smiled sympathetically as they walked past her for she knew just how much they'd been looking forward to the big opening. The madam of the biggest bordello in Calico County was a handsome woman of forty, no longer available to the clients, but still the best looker in the house. Taller than average, Belle had a fine full-bodied figure, generously curved and graceful with deep breasts and flaring hips. Her face seemed arrested in the final smoothness of maturity which comes directly before the lines of experience and age begin to shatter it. Belle's flower-blue eyes could be warm as spring or cold as winter depending upon her mood. She bossed her business and it didn't do for anybody to forget it.

Belle Shilleen had had one great love in her life which she didn't talk about any more and her girls hadn't seen her give a single man so much as a smile of encouragement in months, until good-looking Duke Benedict had stepped elegantly through the doorway a few nights back. Belle looked upon herself as the protector of her brood of pretty hustlers, and they in turn regarded Belle as mother, confidant and confessor all rolled into one.

'Don't fret too much, girls,' she comforted them, following them through into the upstairs parlor which was almost ready for opening night. 'I've never seen the posse yet that didn't run out of steam inside twenty-four hours.'

'Speakin' about steam, Belle honey,' said Kitty. 'When's that there good-lookin' Duke goin' to fix the piano?'

'In the morning,' Belle replied, putting a cigarette in a twelve-inch holder and lighting it over the chimney of an ornate table lamp.

The girls cheered up a little at that. 'Will *he* be stayin' for the openin', Belle?' Kitty wanted to know.

'Most likely.'

The glum expressions faded and the girls returned to work. It didn't seem all that important now whether the posse got back or not, in view of what Belle had just told them. Between them, the girls of Belle Shilleen's 'salon' had encountered just about every breed of man there was. They were authorities on the species. Some men they hated, some they loved, some they despised, some they mothered. Individualists all, they seldom agreed about any man who came their way, drawn by the silent invitation of the rosy red light above Belle's door.

In the case of the gambling man who seemed to have taken such a shine to Belle however, they were unanimous. Of all the men they'd ever met, the good and the bad, the ugly and the comely, rich or poor, winners or losers, liars, frauds, empire-builders or baby-faced cowboys, Duke Benedict, they fully agreed, was unquestionably the most handsome man unhung.

And if Duke Benedict was going to be here Friday night, why, that was about all the guarantee they needed that the night was going to be like the Fourth of July.

SIX

REMEMBER BO RANGLE?

The town clock was striking nine when Sam Fink released his charges and the two tall men stepped out onto the jailhouse porch. It was already hot, and the fierce yellow glare of the sun bouncing off the dusty street didn't do anything for throbbing heads.

Both men had used Sam's razor, and but for the odd bruise or two and a touch of greenish pallor, didn't look too much the worse for wear. Benedict was still the best-dressed man on Johnny Street despite yesterday's clothes and his night in the cells. Brazos by contrast looked just that much more disreputable than when he'd ridden in. The purple shirt had been ripped half off him in the melee last night and some true vandal had stomped his hat, though any worsening of its shape could only have been apparent to him. The big man in fact looked like he'd had an argument with a buzz saw and come out with honors about even.

Bullpup growled good morning from the end of the gallery where somebody had chained him after the brawl last night, drunk as an Irish pig. Brazos growled back and tugged out his packet of Bull Durham and set about building a cigarette with fingers that were almost steady now. Benedict watched him but made no move for his silver cigar case. He wasn't quite ready for that first Havana yet.

It was Benedict who finally ventured to break the sun-baked silence.

'How do you feel, Reb?'

Brazos fired his quirly with a sweep of a lucifer and sucked in a great lungful of smoke. He coughed, spat in the dust then took another deep draw just to show he wasn't about to take any sass from any cigarette.

'How do I feel? I feel like hell is a mile away and all the fences are down.'

'Dry?'

'As a lime-burner's boot.'

'Going to have a pick-me-up?'

'Mebbe later.'

Brazos' tone was rough, his manner surly.

Last night he'd been ready to raise hell forever and drink the whole world dry with his old buddy Duke Benedict. Today he had the grand-daddy of headaches and his mouth felt that at some time during the night, some small, furry animal had made it first his bedroom then his urinal and finally his grave. Added to that was the bitter knowledge that he'd let some clowns get the better of him at the Bird Cage, and to top it off he found himself sharing the morning-after horrors with a high-rolling, light-fingered gambling man who talked like a school teacher and dressed up like a Christmas tree.

Hank Brazos hadn't forgotten Pea Ridge; he never would. But in the hard glare of daylight and sobriety, he knew instinctively that Duke Benedict and he came from opposite ends of the street and were just about as different as two men could be. Duke Benedict would always stick in his mind as the bravest man he'd ever met, but they were a different breed and they could never be anything else. So they'd met unexpectedly and they'd celebrated. So that was that.

He spat in the dust again. 'Stayin' around town?'

'Could be.'

'Then mebbe I'll see you around.'

Benedict nodded, glancing sideways with some distaste at the big figure propping up the gallery. He sensed the change in the relationship, understood it much more quickly and clearly than did Brazos, and welcomed it. Their reunion was well and truly over for Duke Benedict. Last night, with his judgment sadly affected by alcohol he might have considered Brazos as an amusing companion, perhaps even a friend. Today, he saw him as he really was, a brawling illiterate saddle tramp. Pea Ridge, Georgia, seemed a million miles away in the revealing glare of the Kansas sun, distant and unreal. All that was real this hangover morning, was that because of Hank Brazos he felt like something the dogs had had under the house, he'd made a fool of himself, and for one of the rare times in his life, had spent a night in a prison cell.

'Sure,' he said, touching fingers to hat brim as he stepped down from the gallery and headed for his hotel. 'See you around, Reb.'

Brazos watched the tall figure recede. His stormy blue eyes were thoughtful. He'd seen the faint distaste in Benedict's face, realized the gambler had also sensed the great gulf between them, and didn't give much of a damn.

But he was curious, he realized, though with his brain feeling like so much damp cotton wool, he couldn't put his finger on what it was about Benedict, Daybreak, and last night that nagged at him, like an itch he couldn't scratch.

The hell with that. What he needed was a drink.

He stepped out into the full blast of the sun and angled for the Bird Cage, a big shambling man with his shoulders hunched, a torn shirt hanging half off his back, hands hooked in his shell belt and kicking a rusty can before him. He was more than a formidable sight and passers-by stepped warily out of his path, mistaking his scowl of concentration for ferocity.

He gave way for nobody, whether afoot, mounted or on wheels – until the girls dusted by. He stopped in the ankle-deep dust and with his cigarette dangling from his lower lip, hazed a grin at them. They smiled back brazenly as they swept by, and a greenhorn might have thought they owned the town. Brazos knew better. They were young and toughly pretty, dressed in bright silks with painted faces, bleached hair blowing in the wind and paste jewelry glittering around throats and wrists. They sped on down the stem, speaking to none but looked at by all wearing expressions of haughty contempt. He grinned to himself as he saw them swing in at the brick house down Johnny Street. Then he continued on for the saloon.

It was cool and quiet in the Bird Cage with only a smattering of early customers. Last night's wreckage had been pretty well cleaned up, though a boarded-up window and several new bullet holes in the back wall were mute reminders of what had taken place.

And Strom Beecher and Mick Quade were sitting down at a table sipping rye whisky.

Suddenly Hank Brazos was no longer thinking of his thirst. Suddenly, with a hard bright light in his blue eyes, he was thinking only of last night and how a certain pair of rannies had got the best of him only because he'd been drunk, and how hard Quade had hit him with that chair. Their superior cocky looks now were like a red rag to a bull. They thought they had his number. . . .

The hardcases stiffened as he lounged over to the table. Quade's eyes popped as Brazos lifted his glass and drained it at a gulp. With a roar, Quade came up swinging. Brazos smashed him on the bridge of the nose, gripped the edge of the table and flung it aside, scattering bottle and glasses and bringing enraged shouts from Beecher who fell over backwards with his chair and crashed to the floor, still cussing.

Nose streaming claret, Quade crashed in with a big left. Brazos' fist exploded against his jaw and he was down and out. Beecher was still struggling to rise. Brazos helped him up, then jack-knifed him with a rip to the guts and stretched him across Quade with a booming haymaker.

Harp Moody came rushing from out back, hair disheveled, eyes bugging. He gaped at Brazos, then at his bouncers, back to Brazos again.

Brazos grinned and dusted his hands. 'I don't like to have jokers struttin' about the idea they can lick me, Moody,' he explained amiably. 'This straightens things out some. You get the idea?'

Moody wilted. Last night he'd congratulated himself on his triumph. Now it looked like he'd just been lucky. Brazos' wide shoulders, his challenging grin and the two prostrate bouncers were proof of that. Yes, Harp Moody got the idea all right. Brazos was the breed who always came back.

'No hard feelin's, Moody,' Brazos drawled, and feeling a whole lot better, shambled across to the bar where the shaky barkeep was pretending to polish a glass.

Brazos put him at ease with a friendly grin, spun a silver dollar on the zinc top.

'I come in peace, pardner,' he grinned. 'Want to smoke the peace pipe?'

'Huh?'

'Have a drink with me.'

The barkeep went limp with relief. 'Why, sure, Brazos.' He smiled, showing tombstone teeth as he poured whisky. 'For a moment there I thought you were gonna start up where you left off last night.'

'Only got kind of a dim recollection of that there ruckus,' Brazos admitted, fingering back his battered hat to sit precariously at the back of his head. 'Nobody got hurt, did they? I mean, really hurt?'

'No, not all that bad,' replied the barkeep, a lanky

stray with a nasal drip. Then growing confidential, 'Matter of fact, I kinda enjoyed it all.' He snickered. 'No siree, I don't recall seein' as much hell-raisin' in town since Bo Rangle left.'

Hank Brazos lifted his glass, drank deep. The name didn't hit him at first, but when it did it hit him hard.

His glass came down to the bar top, very slowly. 'Did I hear you right, mister? Did you say Bo Rangle?'

The train rolled into the station at Chisolm, panting like a spent stallion. The grimy black clouds from the smoke-stack stretched out for miles fading into the distance until it was nothing more than a faint smudge against the summer sky of Kansas.

The three tall men stepped down stiffly from one of the yellow wooden cars. For a moment they stood together, a part of, yet somehow aloof from the swirl of movement and noise about them. Nobody spoke to them, they spoke to nobody. The three were dressed alike with ankle-length gray dusters covering their trail clothes. They wore the collars of the dusters turned up high, hats tugged down low. The tallest of the three wore his kerchief pulled up over the lower part of his face as if in protection against the dust. From underneath his low hat brim, intent brown eyes cut sharply at a man strolling through the crowd wearing a star. The lawman kept on his way, the tall man grunted, then led the way down to the horsebox.

They paid the railroad conductor, then led their horses down the ramp toting saddles and warbags over their shoulders. The conductor watched them curiously but quickly turned away when the one with the black beard returned his stare. The three men didn't look the kind to appreciate curiosity.

None of the three spoke until they'd ridden clear of the dust and noise of Chisolm. The tallest man then drew his horse to a halt on a timbered saddle, tugging down his kerchief to reveal the sort of long, strong face that once seen wasn't easily forgotten.

'So far so good,' he said, taking a flask from a pocket of the duster and tipping it to his lips.

'How fer from here to Daybreak, boss?' said Dunstan, the man with the black beard.

'Around forty miles.'

'Will we make it by tonight?' queried Glede Skelley, a spare hard man with a yellow moustache.

'Sure, it's easy ridin'.'

The leader put his flask away. Skelley and Dunstan stared south at the rim of the hills that formed the north border of Calico Valley without enthusiasm.

'Cheer up,' the tall man said, noting their uncertainty. 'I'm not plannin' to stay on. I just aim to drop in on openin' night to see how my investment looks, maybe have a drink or two with Belle, then light out. Nothin' to it.'

'That's one thing I've never been able to figure, Bo,' puzzled Dunstan. 'How come you sunk two grand in a brothel?'

'You've got to look to the future, and a bordello's as sound an investment as a man can make this side of the Mississippi,' came the laconic reply. Bo Rangle slapped his reins and used his heels. 'OK, let's cover some miles.

And wipe those looks off your pans, will you? We don't have anythin' to worry about down there. I'm about the last pilgrim Daybreak expects to see tonight or any night.'

They rode on and Skelley's worried frown was gone, but Dunstan continued to brood as the fiery yellow sun climbed the sky. What Bo had said was convincing up to a point, but what Dunstan couldn't figure was why Bo had picked him and Skelley to ride along. Next to Bo himself, they were the top guns in the band at present holed up across the Missouri border. Seemed funny Bo should single them out if it was going to be such a picnic.

Still, he wasn't all that worried. He'd been riding with the boss for two years and knew he wasn't a man to take fool risks. If Bo Rangle said it was safe in Daybreak for them, then that's how it was.

SEVEN

SPROD PLAYS TO WIN

It was an hour after his release from jail when Duke Benedict emerged from his hotel. He'd bathed and changed into a tailored brown suit, watered-silk Prince Albert vest and highly-shined brown dress boots that caught the sun as he walked two doors down Johnny Street and entered the steamy doorway of Willy Wong's laundry.

It was ten minutes before he reappeared, donning his low-crowned gray Stetson. He paused to check his appearance in the laundry window. Satisfied, he took out a cigar, set it alight then strode briskly north along the boardwalk in the direction of Belle Shilleen's.

A pretty girl smiled at him as he passed the wheelwright's. Benedict doffed his hat, flashed his white smile and continued on with the smile still playing about his lips. He was feeling better by the minute. Perhaps another small bourbon at Belle's before going to work on her piano, and he would be one hundred per cent.

'Why, you sure do up well, Yank.'

Benedict came to a dead halt, tugging the cigar from his teeth. Hank Brazos stood leaning lazily in the doorway of an old, disused bakery twenty feet away. The big man straightened and strolled out into the sun, one brown hand hooked in his belt, the other toying with the harmonica dangling from the cord around his neck. Brazos was wearing a big grin that looked somehow smug.

'You being funny?' Benedict said tersely.

'*Me?*' Brazos said innocently. 'Hell no, Yank. Just happened to remark on how damned purty you look. Sure wish I had me a store suit like that there.'

Benedict stared at him closely. There was a mocking quality to Brazos' words, and that smile was plainly phony.

'OK, so you like my rig,' he said shortly, turning to go. 'And now you'll have to excuse me.'

'Goin' along to Belle's?'

Benedict took two strides, propped and glared back. 'What's it to you if I am?'

Brazos shrugged, great slabs of muscle moving beneath the purple shirt that Duke Benedict wouldn't be caught dead in. 'Not a thing I guess, Yank.' And then, as if the idea had only just occurred to him: 'Say, reckon I'll come along with you. That's if you don't have no objections.'

Benedict came back slowly, gray eyes tight. 'Look,

Brazos, we had our fun last night. I enjoyed it, and who knows, maybe someday we'll tie another one on. But right now, I have business to attend to.'

'Sure, sure I understand. Or leastways I reckon I do.' Brazos' face underwent a swift, sober change. 'Your business in Daybreak got anythin' to do with Bo Rangle by any chance, Yank?'

It was suddenly very still in Johnny Street. A dangerous look crossed Duke Benedict's face, then was gone, leaving the sculptured features cold.

'So you know about Rangle?'

'That he's been around these parts? Yeah, I heard tell. Seems kinda funny you never mentioned it last night, Yank.'

'Why should I?'

'I dunno. Mebbe you can tell me.'

Benedict shook his head slowly from side to side. 'Nothing to tell,' he said convincingly. 'I don't know what you're driving at, Reb,' he added, 'and I don't much care. All I know is that I don't have any more time to waste jawboning.'

Brazos screwed his face into a heavy frown as he watched Benedict stride off. He scratched his belly, kicked at a stone and felt the familiar ache in his temples that always came with too much thinking.

He let Benedict go fifty yards, before tilting his hat forward and with his hands thrust deep into his hip pockets, slouched after him.

Ben Sprod's face told its own story as he slowly lowered the field glasses. Wordlessly he passed the glasses to

Frank Piano, then spat on the rocks and tugged out his tobacco caddy. It was hot in the hills where the outlaws had drawn up to rest, even in the shade of the vast cottonwood that landmarked this broad, stony mesa in the Sweet Alice Hills.

There was no trail up here. From the mesa the land descended in wide curves for several hundred feet where it broke against a gaunt rock shoulder that looked like a horse trying to climb into the brassy Kansas sky. The ridge stretched far northward and formed the southern wall of the deep canyon beyond. Sun-bleached flats of buffalo grass swept beyond the canyon, broken by streams lined by willows and cottonwoods. In the distance, so far away that they looked like insects against the whiteness of the plains, rode the posse.

Ben Sprod hadn't believed it was actually the posse when they'd first sighted it as they rode leisurely through the familiar ruggedness of the Sweet Alice Hills. Sure, there'd been rumors for weeks that Daybreak was going to get a big posse out after him as soon as they could get a gunfighter or two to ride with them, but the badmen hadn't really believed it any more than they'd really believed that some gunslick bounty-hunter named Surprising Smith had been signed on by the Daybreak Town Council.

But there was no longer a shadow of doubt now. With the aid of the glasses, Ben Sprod had picked out and identified the figures of Humphrey Carbrook, Dobie Clanton the storekeeper, Jesse Morgan of the stage depot and three or four other familiar faces among the big bunch, but had looked longest and hardest at a small, unfamiliar figure decked out in gunfighter's black.

'Hell's breeze!' Frank Piano said angrily as he studied the riders. 'They're ridin' dead on our tracks from Daybreak, Ben. I said all along it was a crazy idea of yours to go that close to town, even if we was—'

His words were chopped off as Ben Sprod caught him with a vicious backhanded slap across the mouth. The blow almost knocked Piano to the ground. He spat blood, and for a moment his eyes blazed with fury. But he wilted when he saw that hungry look in Sprod's sunken eyes and the way his fingers fanned over the butt of his Colt.

'Sorry, Ben,' he muttered, wiping the back of his hand across his bloody lips. 'I never meant to run off at the mouth.'

Ben Sprod spat between Piano's dusty boots, lips curling in a sneer. He wasn't going to have any tenth-rater saying he'd made a mistake, even if it was as plain as paint that he had. He knew now he shouldn't have gone so close to Daybreak hunting that gunfighter. But how the hell was he to know that they'd finally get around to sending that posse out after them.

'Well, what are we goin' to do, Ben?' Dick Grid asked after a heavy, hot minute. Grid's left arm was strapped wrist to shoulder in bandages and hanging in a black sling. He'd stopped a slug in the elbow in the set-to with Hank Brazos the day before.

'Do we quit the valley?'

'The hell we do,' Sprod shot back.

'But, Ben—'

'But nothin'. This here's my valley and I ain't fixin' to

be choused out by no bunch of plaster-gutted towners callin' theirselves a posse.'

'But damnitall, Ben, our hosses ain't in no condition for a long run.'

'I know that,' the outlaw leader snapped back. Sprod glared at the horses. They were blowing softly through their nostrils and jingling their gear as they rubbed their heads against their legs to mop off the sweat. They'd been ridden hard and badly fed for too long. He didn't figure the posse would last long, but if it did new mounts would be needed.

With sudden decision, he crossed to his horse and mounted up.

'Where to, Ben?' Piano asked as he and Grid followed suit.

'The Circle C Ranch,' said Sprod, cutting a final look down at the posse before heeling away. 'Olan Fletcher runs the best horseflesh in Calico Valley.'

Piano and Grid weren't about to argue with that. But what they couldn't figure was how Sprod meant to talk Olan around. Olan was a cousin of Ben's, but Ben still owed him plenty for horses they'd got before, and Olan had told him straight out he wasn't going to let him have any more until he paid up. And big, tough Olan had sounded like he meant it.

The riders came out of the hills, then angled south-east. They crossed a broad, rolling plain ribboned with chaparral and speckled with beeves. The sun was high when they topped a swale and eyed the Circle C ranch house, shaded by a grove of tall peppercorns. The fans of a windmill on spidery legs whirled lazily and the clanking of the pump sounded faintly in the singing stillness.

They rode in. They spotted Olan Fletcher at work in the horse corrals by the house. Three abreast they crossed the hard-packed sand of the house yard scattering a clutch of fat Dominique hens. Big Olan Fletcher scowled hard when he saw who it was, and the scowl cut even deeper when Ben Sprod told him what they wanted.

'No horses until you pay for the last cavvy, Ben. I made that clear to you afore.'

'There's a posse on our heels, Olan.'

'That ain't no concern of mine.'

Sprod's voice softened as he stepped down. 'You ain't hearing good. Cousin Olan. I want horses. You wouldn't turn your own kinfolk down in time of need, would you?'

'That's the same line of bull dust you handed me last time,' Fletcher said heatedly, big rivers of sweat coursing down his hard, beefy face. 'Cost me three prime saddlers that time. You ain't doin' me again.'

Sprod spread his hands then dropped them at his sides sending up the dust. 'Olan,' he said regretfully, 'you're sure gettin' hard in your old age. Here's your cousin hot and beat and run ragged by a posse and all you can say is—'

'You ain't goin' to make me change my mind, Ben.' Sprod shrugged. 'OK, Olan, but you wouldn't deny a man a cold drink, would you? Do you still keep that barrel of sweet water in the kitchen like you used to?'

Fletcher scowled; then wiped his sleeve across his mouth. 'All right, you can take a drink. But you tell your pards to stay put, Ben. I never did trust that pair of beauties.'

'You heard Cousin Olan,' Sprod said, but as Fletcher turned for the house, he nodded imperceptibly to his henchmen before following.

The water was cold and Sprod let it splash out of his mouth and down his bony chest. Fletcher watched him uneasily, leaning back against the kitchen workbench. His heavy shoulders were tensed and his fingers drummed against the wood.

'Just like old times, Olan,' said Sprod. He hung the water ladle back on its nail above the barrel. 'You recall when my maw used to bring me around and we'd fool in the barn and then come lickin' up here for a nice cool drink?' '

'That was a long time ago, Ben. That was afore you turned killer and thief.'

'Ah, time's made you hard and no mistake, Olan.' Sprod shook his head sadly but there was a steely glint in his sunken eye. 'Never did think I'd live to see the day my own kin would turn so hard agin me.'

A horse whickered from the corrals, followed by a stamp of hoofs. Fletcher started, looked at Sprod, then hurried to the doorway. A curse broke from his lips when he saw Dick Grid and Frank Piano cutting three horses out of the corrals.

'Git away from my hosses!' he roared angrily. He dragged out his gun and pounded down the steps. 'Git out of that corral, you thievin' pair of no-goods.'

Neither man paid him any attention. Fletcher ran twenty yards then stopped in his tracks as a chill of premonition hit him like a blow. He spun in the dust. Ben Sprod's long frame filled the kitchen doorway. Sprod was smiling and he had *his* gun out.

Fletcher's jaw fell open with an audible click as Sprod's gun arm lifted. For a moment as he met the sinister chill of Ben's smile, he knew true fear before rage took over, shaking him like an aspen in a high wind.

'You dirty Judas, Ben!' he shouted and swung up his gun.

Sprod's .45 exploded, the boom of the shot startling the horses in the corrals and setting the hens squawking again.

Olan Fletcher was knocked against a dusty tree trunk with lead in his guts, his face a twisted mask of shock and fury.

'Damn you for a butcherin' bastard, Ben Sprod,' he choked and sent a wild bullet into the roof of the house.

Sprod triggered again and hot lead smashed into Fletcher's knee. His head spinning with agony, the rancher realized he was toying with him. Sobbing and cursing he clutched at the tree trunk and slewed sideways, trying to get behind it. From the kitchen the sound of the big six-gun churning again was like the roar of an avalanche. Cruel lead nails drove into Olan Fletcher's broad back and hammered him into the tree. He stayed transfixed there for a full ten seconds after the gun had fallen silent, then slowly slid down the trunk and rolled onto his back on the hard sand.

Ben Sprod crossed the yard, his shadow a black pool around his boots. He fingered fresh shells into his gun and favored the dead man with nothing more than a half-bored glance as he jingled past the tree to the corrals.

'Always was a hardhead,' was his obituary for Cousin

Olan. 'All right you jokers, let's get our saddles onto these three goers and make some dust.'

There was probably more virtue to be found in the Carbrooks' front parlor that morning than in all the rest of Calico Valley. There was always a lot of virtue about when the Christian Ladies of Daybreak got together, and there was an even bigger roll-up than usual this hot Friday morning. The rumor had gone about that at long last the long-suffering womenfolk of Daybreak were preparing to 'take matters into their own hands.'

Mrs Carbrook's help had finished serving coffee and cakes and Matilda Carbrook herself was doing the talking. This was mostly the case, for not only was she founder and chairwoman of CLOD – an abbreviation the good ladies didn't care for – but she also had an uncommonly loud voice.

That voice was growing louder as the stern and sturdy Mrs Carbrook warmed to her subject. 'It's perfectly obvious that our menfolk will simply not take us seriously,' she declared, not for the first time that morning. 'If they did, they certainly would not have gone gallivanting off after that ridiculous outlaw just at the very time when we need to present a solid, united front against the forces of Satan right here in our fair town.' That brought an enthusiastic chorus of approval. The good ladies weren't really concerned if Ben Sprod went about shooting up stage guards and cowboys. They knew where the real evil lay right enough, and that was about one block west of the Carbrook house right here in Daybreak.

'I called this meeting for a specific purpose,' Mrs Carbrook went on, gaining momentum by the minute.

'And that is to decide whether or not we are going to sit back and watch this ... this monument to Daybreak's shame be officially opened for ... for ... well, you all know what for... tomorrow night, or are we going to stop it?'

'We shall stop it, Matilda!' spinsterish Miss Susie Briggs declared vehemently. 'What that scarlet woman has built there on the corner of Piute Street is a danger to every man and an affront to every God-fearing woman in Daybreak.' Then lapsing into the Biblical as she lifted a furled umbrella high: 'I say this citadel of wickedness must be destroyed lest Daybreak become an American Gomorrah!'

Wild applause, stamping high heels, even an exuberant whistle or two. Standing facing the rows of chairs, it was all Matilda Carbrook could do to suppress a triumphant smile. Things were going far better even than she could have hoped. She hadn't been sure before that her fellow CLOD members felt as strongly about Belle Shilleen's new bordello as she did herself, but their mood this morning was more than convincing.

She lifted her hands for silence and was about to continue her address when her eye was caught by a tall figure walking past the house. Mrs Carbrook's high color turned to brick red as she marched across the room to the window, beckoning them all to come take a look.

'If we needed any more to convince us that things have gone beyond all the bounds of decency here, then that should dispel them,' she declared. 'Do you know who that fellow is? He's a gambling man named Benedict. Each morning for the past three mornings, I've seen him go past here and march straight into that – that place. At least that harlot's other customers were discreet enough to confine their visiting hours to night-time, but now they're going down there in broad daylight.'

The women clucked like so many disapproving hens as they watched the tall, handsome figure. And sure enough, when he reached the Piute Street corner, he crossed over to the big new bordello and went straight inside. 'Disgusting,' gasped Mrs Harp Moody.

'Appalling,' agreed Mrs Jesse Morgan.

'Revolting,' agreed pretty little Hallie Martin, wife of the Reverend Martin. And then a trifle winsomely, 'My, but isn't he a comely gentleman. One can't help wondering why a man like that would want to – need to – oh dear!'

The young woman broke off in confusion, sensing that what she was saying might have sounded a little indelicate. Reproving faces turned to her and she blushed in embarrassment. She was finally saved when Miss Susie Briggs suddenly gasped:

'Look, ladies, there's *another* one!'

The ladies looked. A large, somewhat reprehensible figure was slouching past the picket fence. In sharp contrast to the immaculate Benedict, this stranger to Daybreak looked as if he might have come straight from the cow yard. He wore an impossible purple shirt unbuttoned almost to the waist to reveal a great barrel of a chest which was ornamented by a silver harmonica hanging from a cord around his neck. A battered disaster of a hat sat on the extreme back of his big blond head, and as he walked he was kicking a battered can before him. Had he looked their way, he might have been startled to see a score of pop-eyed women staring out the big window. But his attention seemed fixed on the big brick building on the corner. And as the gambler had done, he ambled across to the bordello as if it was quite the most natural thing in the world and disappeared through the front door.

The timing of Belle Shilleen's two mid-morning clients couldn't have better suited Mrs Carbrook had she planned it that way.

'Well, ladies?' she said ominously, turning away from the window. 'Need any more be said?'

It certainly need not. They'd seen enough, and all that remained now was to work out a plan of action. That took them the rest of the morning, but by the time the meeting was over, two vital decisions had been reached.

The first of these would be implemented if the posse hadn't returned by nightfall. An elected delegation of CLOD members would pay a visit to the bordello to warn Belle Shilleen personally for the last time that they didn't intend to let her go ahead and open her new house for business that night.

The second and more drastic decision concerned the course of action they would follow only if their warning fell on deaf ears. The time for talking and pussy-footing was over, they declared unanimously. If all else failed then they must use force. Husbands, brothers, sons, fiancés, friends all would be brow-beaten and bullied into supporting them, and they would march on Belle Shilleen's bordello to destroy it.

Only little Mrs Hallie Martin timidly wondered if this

perhaps were not a little extreme, but she was shouted down. The worthy ladies of CLOD had blood in their eyes, and as they fell upon the lunch provided by a triumphant Mrs Carbrook with appetites whetted by the prospects of excitement and perhaps violence, there was more than one of them secretly hoping that Belle Shilleen might reject their warning tonight.

For if she did, and if the town's leaders riding with the posse didn't return beforehand, tonight could easily turn out to be the most exciting night in Daybreak's history.

EIGHT

THE SECRET

It was hot enough to make a lizard sweat and even hotter than that down in the hole.

'I'm beat, Mayor,' Flory Rand gasped, leaning his weight on his little saddle shovel. 'Can somebody else take over a spell?'

Standing grim-faced around the deepening grave, Carbrook nodded to Big Henry Peck. Peck took Rand's shovel and got into the hole with Buck Tanner and started to dig. Flory Rand climbed out and sat down against the trunk of the live oak that would be Olan Fletcher's marker. The fat cowboy was panting like a dog running rabbits in mid-summer with the sweat oozing from the flesh on his face and neck and trickling down upon his pale blue shirt turning it several shades darker. He sat there for a while too licked and hot even to speak.

Nobody else spoke either.

The steady thud of the shovels reassured the hens that

had scattered under the building when the posse had come in and they emerged again to stare curiously across at the live oak where all the men were gathered. One of them came to the deep brown stains in the sand near the other tree where Fletcher had fallen. It scratched listlessly then bent its long neck and looked at its scrawls, neither surprised nor angry at not having dug up a worm. Another chicken began singing in the heat, drooping its wings until the tips dragged on the sand. A posse man tossed a rock and the singing ceased.

Finally the hole was deep enough. Four men hefted the sheet-wrapped shape and lowered it in. The shovels worked again. When the grave was filled everybody uncovered while the mayor said the right words.

When Carbrook was through, he replaced his hat and lit a cheroot with fingers that weren't quite steady. He looked at the dark, twisted face of Surprising Smith standing at his elbow, then at the men standing around Olan Fletcher's raw grave.

He said, 'Well, do you still want to head back to town?'

The posse men exchanged silent glances. They were saddle sore, unshaven and weary-eyed. An hour back when they'd paused to spell the horses before reaching the Circle C, some had talked about quitting but the very ones who'd looked the most exhausted then, seemed to be the most grim now after seeing what had happened to Olan Fletcher.

'I say we go on,' Jesse Morgan said abruptly. It had been Morgan who'd been first to suggest they quit.

A rumble of hard voices rose in agreement. By butchering Olan Fletcher that way, Ben Sprod had done himself a bad turn. The brutal murder had reminded every man there that they couldn't quit now that they were finally camped on his trail.

Carbrook grunted in approval and mounted up. They followed him out across the yard, once again scattering the fat hens. Once clear of the yard, Surprising Smith rode out ahead to pick up the killers' sign once again.

'You know, my daddy was a preacher of sorts,' Sweet Shirley confided.

'Do tell,' Brazos, said noncommittally.

'Yeah . . .the sort to make you want to throw your Bible away.'

'I know the sort.'

Silence fell again, the silence that comes to all bordellos in summer's midday heat, whether they be rough little clapboard shacks, or a fine new palace of sin like Belle Shilleen's.

The ground floor parlor where Brazos sat taking ease from the outside heat with six of Belle's girls was quite the plushest room he'd ever been in. Some thirty feet long by twenty wide, it was carpeted wall-to-wall with a rich red Brussels pile that shone with a soft luxurious gleam under the lamps that burned as bright at noon as at midnight. There were velvet-covered settees, plush divans, fine drapes and curtains. Large gilt-framed paintings of bouncing, naked ladies adorned dark blue walls, and in pride of place in one corner stood the new steam piano.

Until today, one piano had been much the same as another to Hank Brazos, but not now. He knew all about Belle Shilleen's piano, for he'd just spent the entire morning helping Benedict erect the pipes that would make it go.

Benedict had been somewhat annoyed when Brazos had arrived at Belle's almost on his heels three hours back, but once he realized he meant to stay around, he'd promptly put him to work. The work had comprised laying pipes from the boiler-room of Belle's old establishment next door, across the backyard and under the floor of the new building to connect up with the piano's fittings. Belle had intended going to the expense of setting up a steam machine inside the new premises, but Benedict, with some professional advice from laundryman Willy Wong who knew all about steam, had devised this alternative.

They'd stoked up the sturdy boilers next door after they got the pipes linked up and now the piano worked perfectly. As long as the boiler fire was kept going, the piano would play twenty-four hours a day if needed and would save Belle the considerable cost of employing a player. That saving, Benedict estimated, would pay for the cost of the piano within a year.

Brazos hadn't minded the work, but the whole business had made him even more curious about why Benedict was going out of his way to do so much for Belle Shilleen. If Benedict were about right now he'd try and find out, but while he'd been sluicing off the sweat of his labor, in the tub out back, Duke and Belle had disappeared upstairs.

Seated rather gingerly on an ornate little chair that he wasn't quite sure was up to holding him safely, Brazos glanced up at the clock above the gleaming bar which ran the full length of one wall. It was nearly one. They'd been up there a hell of a long time.

He turned to Shirley lounging nearby, almost dressed in something made of filmy chiffon. 'They still upstairs?'

'Guess so, big boy.'

He looked at the ceiling. 'What the hell they doin' you reckon?'

If he'd thought twice before saying that he wouldn't have said it. He realized his mistake when all the girls laughed. 'Now what do you think they're doing, big boy?' Floralee said huskily. 'Playing blackjack maybe?'

They laughed afresh at Floralee's wit. Draped limply but alluringly about the beautiful new room in various stages of dress or undress, each one of the six girls was quite attractive – something that was by no means usual in places of this nature. There was Kitty Kellick, a tall and slender girl from Ohio, Mexican Rita with slumberous eyes and an enchanting accent, redheaded and curvaceous Sweet Shirley, little blonde Floralee from the East, wide-eyed Babby Betty seventeen years old if she was that, and the prettiest of them all, long-legged Gypsy. The girls weren't expecting any clients at this time of day and normally would be resting upstairs so as to be fresh for tonight. But it was hot upstairs, and besides that, Hank Brazos was down here.

Duke Benedict's 'friend' intrigued the employees of Belle Shilleen's. He was nowhere near as handsome as Duke Benedict and he had no more smooth manners then a hen has teeth. Even so, each girl present was disturbingly aware of the aura of vitality he seemed to radiate. Hank Brazos might be rough around the edges, but the girls of Belle Shilleen's found those shoulders quite fascinating, the half-innocent, half-wicked blue eyes disturbing, and something exciting just in the way he talked, real lazy and deep like that, way down in the chest.

Throughout the morning, particularly when he'd been working out the back without his shirt, several of the girls had attempted to entice him to take a break upstairs. Brazos had declined amiably enough, and though he'd convinced them that he wasn't here looking for romance, they were still enjoying just sitting around looking at him.

At another time Hank Brazos might have been more susceptible to so much temptation. After all it wasn't every day a saddle tramp found himself surrounded by such vast areas of plump, soft flesh, alluring eyes, red lips and low, husky voices with the devil in them. But today he had other things on his mind – like what in hell Benedict was up to here?

Another ten minutes passed. Brazos began to get restless as he always did when too long indoors. He finally excused himself with a grunt and went out. He walked down the red-carpeted hallway to the back porch, leant against the wall and built himself a smoke.

He was half-way through his cigarette when long-legged Gypsy followed him out. The girl studied him thoughtfully as he stood with one scuffed boot propped up behind him, then crossed to the little white-painted railing and leant gracefully back against it.

'A penny for them, big boy?'

'Huh?'

'Your thoughts . . . you know?'

Brazos puffed on his weed, didn't reply. He wasn't in a talking mood but that didn't seem to worry her any.

He soon found out why; Gypsy had something on her mind.

'What sort of friends are you and good-lookin' Duke, big boy?' she said suddenly.

That jolted him out of his broody mood. 'How's that again, Gypsy?'

Smooth shoulders shrugged. 'You and Duke Benedict. You said earlier that you and him are old friends.'

'Well, mebbe I didn't exactly mean old friends. Let's just say we know each other.'

'Oh.' Gypsy's face fell.

'What's wrong with that?'

'Oh nothin' much I guess. I just figured that if you and Duke were good friends I might . . .' Her voice trailed away.

'Might what?' Brazos persisted, crossing to her. He could see she was clearly troubled about something. 'What's on your mind, Gypsy?'

The girl eyed him thoughtfully for a long moment before speaking with sudden determination.

'Maybe I'm speakin' out of turn, big boy, but I reckon somebody's got to. We all like good-lookin' Duke, and I guess we like the cut of your rig, too. I don't want to see either of you boys get yourselves hurt, specially when you don't know what you're lettin' yourselves in for.'

'You still ain't makin' sense, little gal.'

'All right, I'll try and make sense then. Good-lookin' Duke has taken a shine to Belle, right?'

'Seems so.'

'It sure does. Well the truth of it is, Belle's already got herself a feller.'

'She has? Benedict never said nothin' about that as I recall.'

'I reckon he wouldn't have, on account he wouldn't know.'

'You mean Belle's kept it to herself? Well, that's a lady's right I guess.'

'You still don't get the idea, big boy.' Gypsy's pale, pretty face was very serious now as she looked up at him. 'You see Belle's old beau is a badman, a gunman and a killer. If he was to show up kinda unexpected, and find Belle and your friend Duke holdin' hands, he'd just as likely let fly first and ask questions later. Now do you get me?'

Brazos certainly did. He looked up at the ceiling, then said, 'You want that I warn Benedict off?'

'Well, he might take notice of you, if you're pards.'

Brazos rubbed his jaw. 'I don't know if he would or not. The Yank don't scare easy. Say, what's this badman's handle anyway, Gypsy?'

The girls' eyes dropped quickly. 'I don't see how that's important.'

'It could be if I am to convince the Yank he's treadin' dangerous.'

Gypsy looked up at him levelly. 'OK, I guess you're right, big boy. But keep this to yourself, will you? This is somethin' only the girls really know about and it wouldn't do Belle or anybody else any good to have the whole town know the truth.' She took a deep breath. 'Belle's feller is

Bo Rangle, big boy. No doubt you've heard about him?'

Hank Brazos had a brief impression of time standing still. He lifted his cigarette to his mouth to disguise his reaction to her words, but his hand was not quite steady.

'Some boyfriend, Gypsy,' he said softly. 'Tell me about it.'

'Well, you understand I'm only confidin' in you so's you'll try and get Duke to ease off Belle, don't you, big boy? You won't spread it around?'

'You can trust me, Gypsy.'

'Well, Bo and Belle got to be lovers during the war. After it was over, Bo came back to rest up here a spell. He had money and he and Belle decided to go into partnership and build a real bordello that'd give Belle security and Bo a solid investment.'

Brazos couldn't help a fleeting smile. Not everybody would regard a sporting house as a solid investment.

'Well, they'd just got started,' Gypsy continued, 'when things turned sour and the army ran Bo out of the country. Belle was good and mad of course and went right ahead with the buildin' as much to spite Daybreak as anythin' else I guess. She really was sweet on Bo.'

'Was?'

'Well, you see Bo ain't so much as even wrote her a line in I don't know how long, and I know Belle's real hurt about it. Matter of fact I got me an idea she's gone cold on Bo, but that don't mean he won't show up again. Nobody knows when Bo Rangle's liable to show up any place, so I reckon you can see why you better talk with Duke. I'd of tipped him off before but I doubt if he'd pay me any heed. But he might listen to a friend.' She frowned at him. 'Say . . . are you OK, Hank?'

Brazos didn't reply, for in that moment he could see the whole thing as it was. Suddenly he knew just exactly why Duke Benedict was holding hands with Belle Shilleen and rigging up steam for her goddamn piano and all the rest. He saw it crystal clear and it hit him, where he lived, like a kick in the groin.

'Well I'll be teetotalling damned,' he breathed, looking up at the ceiling. 'That damn Yank. So that's his game.'

'What do you mean, big boy?' Gypsy said in perplexity. '*What* game?'

'Never you mind, Gypsy,' he said, patting her shoulder. 'You've done the right thing, tellin' me what you have about Bo Rangle.'

'You're goin'?' Gypsy looked surprised as he went down the steps. 'But what about Duke and—?'

'I'll see him later, Gypsy,' he told her, conscious that he had to get away by himself for a time and figure things out. He slouched across the yard and added, with a hard grin, 'You can bet on that.'

NINE

A GAME FOR TWO PLAYERS

Duke Benedict donned vest and coat and left the room silently, so as not to disturb the sleeping Belle Shilleen. He closed the door softly, sighed, then headed for the stairs, adjusting his cravat. Strange what a man was prepared to do to get what he wanted, he mused, going down the stairs.

But the trouble was, he still hadn't got what he was after. Belle was still playing coy about Bo Rangle, and it was beginning to annoy him.

The stairway opened into the front parlor. From the doorway, he looked around for a purple shirt. Brazos wasn't there, just Bob French, the ferrety little barkeep, polishing his glasses, and a couple of bored-looking girls, Floralee and Gypsy Jones.

He didn't want to see Brazos. Quite the contrary. But

he'd been so sure he'd find him waiting for him down here that he was curious enough to ask after him.

'He went back up town,' Gypsy supplied, a little strangely, Benedict thought.

'Reckon we must have been borin' him,' Floralee opined, with a suggestion of wounded professional pride.

Benedict nodded and went out. This morning he'd thought that Brazos, with suspicions aroused, might mean to dog him every minute. It seemed now that that was not the case, and that was a bit of a break. Benedict was having problems enough without the big Reb adding to them.

The rooftops of Daybreak shimmered in the heat haze as the gambler headed along Johnny Street. It was mid-afternoon and the orange glare of the sun after the cool gloom of Belle's room started his head to throbbing again. The back of his head was still tender where he'd hit the floor of the Bird Cage last night in that most undignified ruckus, and he was still a trifle overhung. All this added to his failure to make appreciable headway with Belle, was making him feel testy.

But if there was anything Duke Benedict knew better than another, it was that a little romance invariably bucked him up when he was feeling low, and his thoughts were on romance now as he headed for the Bird Cage. Rather convenient, Mr Surprising Smith taking off with the posse, he mused. He wondered how they were getting on with the chase. He was a little surprised that they hadn't run out of steam by this, and come home.

His spirits rose the moment he stepped inside the saloon. He'd been thinking of her all day long, even while entertaining Belle, and there she was. The sight of long silken legs crossed, a black feather boa slung gracefully around slender shoulders and a warming change of expression when she saw him walking towards her stopped his headache dead in its tracks.

'Why, good afternoon, Duke. Funny, but I was just sitting here thinking about you. Can I buy you a drink?'

'Nobody as impossibly beautiful as you can ever buy Duke Benedict a drink,' he said, taking off his hat with a flair that made Honey Smith's fickle heart beat fast. 'Barkeep!' he called. 'A bottle of your best bourbon and two glasses.'

Her lips were like wine, and he simply had to taste them again.

'You're a very forward man, Duke baby,' she murmured, running a slender finger down his jawline. 'Has anybody ever told you that before.'

'Never,' he assured her as they headed for the stairs that led to the rooms above. 'Most women of my acquaintance in fact, complain that I'm a little shy and backward.'

She laughed deliciously, hiccupped, laughed again. Twilight was falling outside and it was gloomy in the rear passageway of the saloon. They'd spent two very pleasant hours together over their bourbon and the day wasn't over yet. He'd promised Belle he'd be at her place tonight, but that was in the future. This was now, the very romantic present. . . .

They almost stumbled over the big figure seated on the bottom stair. Honey shrieked. Benedict grabbed a gun, then let it go as he recognized the big figure uncoiling to his feet.

'Why howdy-do there, Mrs Smith, ma'am. And howdy-do to you, Yank.'

Duke Benedict let fly with a couple of expletives he most definitely hadn't picked up at college.

'What in hell do you think you're playing at, Brazos?' he snarled. 'You're liable to stop a slug, bobbing up on a man like that.'

'You snuck up on me, Yank,' Brazos pointed out. 'Sorry if I scared you any.'

'You didn't scare me,' Benedict snapped back. 'What the sweet Judas are you doing here anyway?'

'Waitin' for you. I seen you two sittin' inside there billin' and cooin', and I had me a hunch that sooner or later you'd be comin' this way.'

Honey Smith giggled, just a little drunkenly. 'Say, he's cute, Duke baby. Don't you think he's cute?'

Benedict did not. He thought rather that Hank Brazos was a Grade A horse's ass, but with a lady present, could hardly say so. What he did say was:

'You're wearing me thin, Johnny Reb. You're making it harder every time I see you to remember that we fought side by side once. I'll put it to you plain. Get out of my hair and damn well stay out.'

'Sorry I can't do that,' Brazos said laconically. 'Matter of fact I've got to talk to you, Yank. Right now.'

'The hell, you say.'

'It's about Belle Shilleen, Yank.' A deliberate pause, then, 'About Belle and her old boyfriend as a matter of fact.'

Duke Benedict swore softly. 'So you know?'

'That's right, Yank. At least some of it. Now do we talk

in front of Mr Surprisin' Smith's little bride, or do we talk private?'

'Let's go,' said Benedict abruptly.

'Duke baby,' the girl protested, 'you're not going off and leaving little Honey all alone, are you?'

That's exactly what Duke Benedict was going to do. But he was anything but happy about it, and by the time he'd escorted her upstairs, and come back down and walked out into the saloon's lamplit backyard with Brazos, the gambler's temper was climbing towards boiling point again.

'All right, Johnny Reb,' he snapped. 'You want to talk, so talk.'

Brazos was very sober. 'All right, Yank, I will.' He licked a cigarette into a neat cylinder and set it between his teeth, the blue eyes hard and accusing. 'Let's see how I've got it figured, Benedict. At Pea Ridge you got yourself a sniff of two hundred thousand bucks in gold and as soon as the war finished you set out after the gold to see if you could pick up the scent again. Right so far?'

'You're doing the talking,' Benedict said coldly, around a freshly-lit cigar. 'I'm listening.'

'OK, well listen good then. You're a smart man, Yank, you got book-learnin'. You find out that Bo Rangle's been around these parts so you drift down here and start sniffin' about. You're lookin' for a lead on him and you find out that Belle Shilleen was his old sweetheart. So what do you do? You take up with Belle and I'll bet my saddle you're pumpin' that girl for all you're worth tryin' to get a lead on Rangle.' A match burst into life on Brazos' thumbnail and set fire to his cigarette. He dragged deeply, exhaled towards the stars that were beginning to show point by point in the night sky. 'Right?'

Duke Benedict's handsome face looked calm enough in the lamplight, but underneath he'd been jolted. He'd figured Hank Brazos was a dumb saddle bum, and Hank Brazos had just proved Benedict had sized him up wrongly.

'Right?' Brazos prompted again.

Benedict let the tension run out of him. He was a good gambler. He knew to a nicety when he could get away with a bluff and when he couldn't. This was one of those times when bluffing or lying wouldn't do any good.

So he put his cards on the table face up. 'Why. . . right I guess, Johnny Reb.'

Brazos nodded gravely to himself. He'd been pretty sure what was going on when Gypsy had told him about Belle Shilleen and Bo Rangle, but he'd needed Benedict's admission to be certain. Now he was.

A cool night wind was rising, stirring the dust of the yard and moaning in the dark pines of the vacant lot next door with a sound like a woman crying, and Brazos was reminded of another night when a cold wind had risen to blow away the gunsmoke and the smell of death from a shell-pocked ridge in Georgia. It was kind of a shame he brooded, that he couldn't have just gone on recalling the Yank like he'd been that day. A pity he couldn't have just remembered him as the bravest man he'd ever met, and not know him now as a man hungry for gold and likely ready to do anything to get it.

'Well?' Benedict snapped as the silence stretched out.

'What's the next play, Reb? Or can I guess?'

'Guess away.'

'You want in. You want a cut.'

Benedict was way wide of the mark. But Brazos didn't let on.

'You really reckon you can track that gold down, Yank?'

'I wouldn't be here if I didn't.'

'Well, I reckon you're sure onto somethin', Yank. What d'you reckon is a fair split, then? Fifty-fifty?'

Benedict's face twisted in a sneer. 'So . . . I guessed right. All that high-flown talk about that gold belonging to the South and what a true-blue honest man you are! So much hogswill! Why, you're just as hungry as me, and hypocritical to boot.'

Brazos' shoulders shrugged and the breeze blew a brief gust of sound through the harmonica on his chest. He grinned and tried to look avaricious.

'Amazin' how the thought of two hundred thousand in hard gold can change a man's thinkin', ain't it? Well, what do you say? We ride double?'

'I say go to hell. I'm not taking in any partners.'

'Seventy-five, twenty-five?'

Another negative came to Duke Benedict's lips but died there. He found himself looking at Hank Brazos in a new light. Before Daybreak he'd known all about the man's courage and fighting ability. Now he also knew that Brazos was a whole lot smarter than he looked, and added to that, Brazos now knew what he was up to. Maybe his proposition was worth thinking about. Maybe he could use a partner in what would likely be a long and dangerous hunt for that gold. Brazos could prove a big asset in the hunt, and when they'd found the gold, if he couldn't out-smart him for his cut, he was slipping. . . 'I'll think about it,' he decided.

'Fair enough, Yank.' Brazos exhaled twin streams of smoke from his nose and grinned boyishly. 'But you won't try nothin' cute, will you, Benedict? Like tryin' to cross me up and takin' off on your lonesome. Mebbe I forgot to tell you afore, but I'm the best blue-eyed sign-reader west of the Mississippi, even if I do say so myself. You get my meanin?'

Benedict got it. He was being told that if he didn't take Brazos as his partner, which was bad enough, then he'd have him dogging his trail all over – which no doubt would be a damn sight worse.

'But I don't figure it, Yank. It's nigh to six months since Rangle's Raiders run off with that gold at Pea Ridge. It stands to reason there wouldn't be much of it left by now, don't it?'

'Sure – if he'd gotten away with it. But everything points to the idea that Rangle didn't get clear with the gold. He ran into Northern troops in Missouri the day after Pea Ridge, got badly mauled but apparently got away – travelling light. I've since talked with men who rode with them. They didn't get Rangle, but they were able to tell me a few interesting things about the chase, and the most significant thing I learned was that the marauder was travelling light.'

'Light? You mean he didn't have the gold?'

'That's my guess. Everybody seems to believe he cached the gold in Missouri some place and would head back to get it when things quietened down. When I heard about this, I kept on his scent until it finally led me right here to Daybreak.'

Brazos nodded to himself again, satisfied that Benedict's story carried the ring of truth. He lit his smoke and said quietly. 'Well, do we team up, Yank?'

'I said I'd think about it, and that's all I'm promising. And now, if there's nothing else on your so-called mind, I've got things to do.'

Brazos took no offence. 'Sure, off you go, Yank.' Then as the gambler turned to leave, 'You goin' down to Belle's now?'

'Later on. Right now I have some unfinished business to attend to.' His glance drifted to the saloon's upstairs lights.

'It ain't no put-in of mine, Yank, but ain't it kind of a chancy business, skylarkin' about with that proddy little bounty-hunter's bride?'

Benedict smiled, the first genuine smile in the past hour. 'It's the risk that makes it exciting, sometimes.'

'Well, it's your hide.' They moved across the yard together. 'But you'll be showing up at Belle's later on?'

'Sure, I wouldn't miss opening night.'

'Me neither I guess, looks like being some shindig. That's unless them Christian Ladies stir up a ruckus – you hear anythin' about that?'

'Yeah, I did. Seems like one heck of a joke to me, a bunch of fat old ladies causing trouble. But Belle seems to think they might mean it. Matter of fact she made me promise to be there tonight in case trouble breaks out. She gave me the idea that if I do show up tonight and things are still OK come morning, then she might, just might, give me the lead I'm after on Rangle.'

'You reckon what she'd tell you would be the truth?' Brazos asked as they reached the outside stairs leading to the upper floor. 'I mean, if she's sweet on Rangle, she ain't likely to spill his whereabouts is she?'

'I have a hunch she's not sweet on him any longer. Sure, she was when the Army chased him out of the valley, but Belle hasn't heard a word from Rangle since he hauled his freight out of here. She feels he deserted her and she's sour. She knows what I want from her and she's hinted she might tell me what I want to know. I reckon that in itself is proof the romance is over.'

Benedict started up the stairs, adding confidently, 'She'll tell me what I want to know right enough, and it'll be the truth. I'm sure of it.'

'Well, if you're sure, I'm sure.' Brazos tipped his hat. 'Well, see you down at Belle's later on then – partner.'

'We're not partners yet, Reb,' Benedict's voice drifted down. 'I just said I'll think about it.'

'You can't really afford to turn me down, the way I see it, Yank,' Brazos called back, slouching towards the corner. 'Not three for you and one for me, you can't. . . .' Brazos laughed as he disappeared in the gloom between the saloon and the store, just to reassure Benedict what an easy-going fellow he really was at heart. But the laughter vanished as if it had never existed as he strode through the darkness, and his big fist punching into his palm made a noise like a kicked box.

'Three for you and one for me – like hell, Yank! If we luck onto that gold you won't be gettin' one plugged cent's worth out of it and neither will I. That there gold, if it ain't been spent or lost already, don't belong to you or me or Rangle or nobody else. It belongs to the South, mister, and the South's a-goin' to git it!'

He was greeted with a surly growl of recognition by Bullpup who was waiting for him on the gallery of the Bird Cage. Brazos delivered the hound an absent-minded poke in the ribs with his boot in response and was heavily conscious of the great change that had taken place inside him in the past couple of hours. In that short time he'd become a man with a purpose in life. And that purpose was to retrieve the Confederate gold any way he could.

He was well aware that he wasn't any nobler than the next man, as he turned away from the alley, and with Bullpup at his heels, made his way slowly towards the hotel to get ready for the night's fun and games, but his sweet-faced old ma and his iron-jawed old pa had sure enough made a good job of teaching him the difference between right and wrong. It was as clear in his mind as anything could be that that gold his brave boys had fought and died for at Pea Ridge still belonged to the South – and to the solitary fading hope of the South exiled in Mexico, General Nathan Forrest. And that's who it would go to, if it turned up. It sure as hell wouldn't go to keep any dandy, womanizing, gunslick Yankee gambling margin cigars and silk vests for the rest of his life.

Not if Hank Brazos could help it, by Judas!

He was almost to the hotel when he turned at the sound of long-striding steps. His blond brows went up in surprise.

'Yank? What?'

'She was asleep – thanks to the time I wasted gabbing to you,' Duke Benedict snapped, going right past him and stomping up the hotel steps.

Brazos grinned. 'Hard luck, Yank.' He winked down at Bullpup. 'Sure is heartbreakin' to see such a nice feller miss out.'

TEN

ALONG THE ARROWHEAD

Ben Sprod spun on his heels at the click of a six-gun hammer.

A curse ripped from the battered outlaw's lips when he saw what Dick Grid was going to do. Taking one long stride, he knocked the gun down, then punched Grid to the side of the head and knocked him down. The crippled horse screamed again. Still cursing, Sprod whipped out his hunting knife and cut the beast's throat.

His tongue mourning after a lost tooth, Grid staggered dustily to his feet, his eyes glazed with pain and surprise.

'What in hell did you go and do that for, Ben?' he demanded querulously, 'I was only a-goin' to put your hoss out of its misery.'

'I know what you were goddamn goin' to do, dammit! You were goin' to let that gun off and bring that posse hammerin' straight for us after we been runnin' our guts out all day tryin' to shake 'em off.'

A stupid look crossed Dick Grid's meaty face as he realized what he'd almost done. When Ben's horse had put its foot in a gopher hole and broken a leg, it had been instinctive for him to want to put the animal out of its misery. It was lucky Ben still had enough wits to stop him, even though he'd been knocked half-silly in the fall.

Maybe it was lucky, but right at the moment Ben Sprod considered himself anything but. In fact Ben couldn't recall when his luck had ever been worse. It had been unlucky enough just to have that posse sticking to their trail like a burr, but now with only two horses between the three of them, things were looking plenty grim.

The accident had occurred on the southern bank of the Arrowhead River which ran the entire length of Calico Valley. They were almost at the end of the good rangeland. To the south and west now lay the badlands which cupped that end of the valley before giving way to the mountains. North across the Arrowhead lay hardscrabble ranching country with dry and sun baked brown hills rolling off into the distance.

Ben Sprod sucked a lacerated finger and looked west. The sun, misshapen and red had been resting on the jagged spine of the Dinosaur Mountains just before the horse fell. Now it was gone and the red and gold of the sky where Bighorn Pass notched through the black range was fading down like an old fire.

The evening wind came up from the south east out of Deaf Smith County raising the dust off the Sweet Alice Hills and spreading it across the darkening sky. Not a sign of a cloud, the outlaw noted. Tonight the full moon would rise and it would be as easy for a posse to follow sign as by daylight. Luck? It seemed he was damned near fresh out of that mighty valuable commodity.

Grid and Piano grew restless. They wanted to be on their way again, but knew that this look on Sprod's face was his thinking look, so didn't interrupt.

Finally Sprod said, 'The old Star 40 ranch house in Cripple Canyon – it still standin'?'

'Was last time I was down that way,' Frank Piano supplied.

'Right, we'll hole up there for the night,' Sprod decided and crossed to Dick Grid's horse. 'You two double up. C'mon, let's get movin'.'

Sprod's henchmen exchanged an alarmed look, and as Grid got up behind him Piano said, 'Ain't that kinda risky, Ben? I mean Cripple Canyon ain't but a few miles from Daybreak, for one thing. And for another, what's to stop the posse readin' our sign right up to the damned door?'

Ben Sprod swore again, not viciously this time, but wearily. Sometimes he wondered if they'd know how to wipe their noses without him.

'We ain't goin' to ride clear across and leave 'em tracks a blind man could follow in the dark, stupid.' He flung a bony hand at the badlands. 'We'll lay a false trail down there, and we'll lay it so good we'll be able to get a full night's rest for our horses while they're runnin' themselves into the ground. Come sun-up then, it's gonna be one mighty weary posse with nothin' more in mind than gettin' home and soakin' their blistered backsides. Let's go.'

He jabbed his heels and the horse swung away. Hipping around in the saddle as they climbed a crest, Ben Sprod could plainly see the posse men's dust even as the shadows of night engulfed Calico Valley.

'Why don't you haul your fat freight, sister?'

'How dare you!'

'I dare right enough. If you and your bunch of blue-nosed hypocrites have got the brass-bound nerve to come down here and threaten me on my own door stoop, then I've certainly got the nerve to tell you what you can do with your big fat threats – sister.'

Mrs Matilda Carbrook, red as a turkey gobbler, turned to see if the rest of the delegation had heard what this impossible woman had said to her. All looked suitably horrified, with the possible exception of the Reverend Martin. The Reverend Martin was staring up at the upper balcony where six half-naked girls had appeared to watch the fun. The Reverend was wearing a most un-reverend look. Martin's wife saw Mrs Carbrook's glare. She nudged her husband and immediately his fatuous expression was replaced by one more suitable for the occasion.

'Disgusting!' he snorted down his long, wet nose. 'Quite disgusting.'

'Ahh, your mother sleeps in outhouses!' tough Kitty Kellick called down from the balcony, and Sweet Shirley chimed in an invitation to the Reverend to come up and join the fun.

That was more than enough for Mrs Carbrook. Puffing herself up like a tickled toad, she fired her parting shot.

'I had hoped you would listen to reason, Miss Shilleen,' she told the richly curved proprietress, who was standing with one hand resting on a flaring hip, the other holding a cheroot in an amber holder. 'I had hoped you would not force us to use drastic measures to close down this monument to the devil, before it lured the first innocent young man into perdition. I should have known better, I should have realized that you are too steeped in the ways of wickedness to—'

Mrs Carbrook broke off abruptly, sensing that she had lost her listener's attention. Turning, she saw why.

The gambling man, Duke Benedict, was coming up the walk with his hat in his hand and smiling at the delegate ladies – and horror of horrors, some of them were actually smiling back!

'Well, what's all this?' Benedict said to Belle, coming up the steps. He flashed Mrs Carbrook a wicked grin. 'Recruiting, Belle?'

For a moment Matilda Carbrook forgot to be incensed at the fellow's tasteless attempt at wit. For dressed up like a Broadway actor in a beautifully tailored dark blue suit and with his thick dark hair brushed high in an immaculate pompadour, Duke Benedict was the most breathtakingly handsome man Mrs Carbrook had ever laid eyes on. So handsome in fact that he actually took her breath away for a moment, but when she recovered she was angrier than before.

'Sir,' she told him, 'your wit, it would seem, is on a par with your morals.' Then she swung back to Belle. 'Goodnight to you then, Miss Shilleen. I only regret that we could not reach some agreement, and I can assure you that before this night is over, you will have full cause to regret it also. Come, ladies.'

She led them for the gate at a march. They followed her looking grim, with the possible exception of the Martins. The Reverend was sneaking one last look at the girls upstairs while his pretty little wife looked glumly back over her shoulder at Benedict.

Just as they reached the gate, hoofs drummed down Johnny Street and six riders slewed in at the hitch rack and jumped down. They were the boys from the Big 6 Ranch, wild young hellions full of fun and in town for the opening. Their noisy arrival spurred the CLOD ladies off at top speed, and Belle Shilleen laughed at Benedict's elbow, watching them go.

'Well, I don't think Mrs Matilda Carbrook will be back in a hurry, Duke.'

Benedict nodded soberly in response to the noisy greetings of the Bar 6 Boys as they tromped inside to be welcomed with squeals of delight by the girls. 'I wouldn't be too sure about that, Belle.'

Belle looked at him sharply. 'How do you mean?' Benedict was looking thoughtfully up Johnny Street the way the delegation had gone. 'Just a hunch I guess. But I've seen women like that stir up more trouble than a fox in a chicken coop before. Sure, they might be a bunch of blue-stockings and perhaps even a bit ridiculous, but they just might be dangerous too.'

'Oh bosh!' the woman said, linking her arm through his. 'If a bunch of old biddies is all I have to worry about, then I don't have much. Come on, let's go inside, it sounds like things are warming up.'

They turned for the door, as boot heels sounded on the walk. The couple halted in the doorway as Hank

Brazos came up the path. The big drifter as usual was wearing his demoralized memory of a hat perched right on the extreme back edge of his skull. He'd just shaved and bathed and his bronzed face shone with good health, cleanliness and amiability. He still sported levis, the leather shotgun chaps and battered boots, but in concession to the occasion, he'd put on a fresh shirt. 'Howdy-do, Miss Belle, Yank.'

Belle Shilleen smiled warmly but Benedict winced. 'Let me guess. You've got a whole satchetful of those shirts?'

Detecting a hint of criticism, Brazos looked down at his brand new purple shirt. It looked great to him and he said so. And then, 'What do you say, Miss Belle?'

'I think it's a lovely shirt, Hank,' Belle assured him, taking his arm also. 'I think you *both* look very, very handsome.'

Brazos beamed even more broadly and Duke Benedict looked heavenwards. Sometimes Benedict paused to wonder what his Boston banker father and his socialite mother would say if they could see him. Now was one of those times, as he stood here on the gallery of a brand new bordello arm-in-arm with the madam and a saddle tramp wearing a shirt that would certainly get a man arrested in any civilized town. Still, if he'd wanted the sedate dignified life, he'd have stayed in Boston and would not have come West looking for wealth and excitement, he had to remind himself, and forced a smile.

'Thank you very much, Belle, and all I can say in response is that you look uncommonly fetching yourself. Shall we go in?'

They went in. The steam piano was going full blast, beating out *Blue Tailed Fly*. Mexican Rita and Sweet Shirley were dancing with a couple of the cowhands and Bob French was already pouring drinks. Some half-dozen towners had already come discreetly in the back way and the big hew parlor was filled with color and music, noise and laughter. Gypsy left a cowboy at the bar immediately she sighted Brazos and came silkily across the room, rolling her hips, to lead him out onto the dance floor. Duke Benedict kissed Belle Shilleen on the cheek, Floralee squealed as a naughty cowboy slipped her blouse off one shoulder to reveal a round, creamy breast and the *Blue Tailed Fly* roller stopped and immediately *Oh Susannah* began.

The big night was under way.

They watered their mounts at the river where they'd found the outlaw's dead horse. Mayor Humphrey Carbrook jerked his horse's head out of the water after a minute so he wouldn't get too much too quick. Around them the Arrowhead was a trembling sheen under the moon and the trees soared high against the sky, light-streaked where the wind turned the leaves. He turned his head back up to the bluffs at the sound of hoofs. Surprising Smith rode into sight and reined in, silhouetted against the new-risen moon.

Carbrook looped his reins over his arm and trudged up the slope, the others following. Surprising Smith swung down and stretched his small body to ease the stiffness, then spoke in response to Carbrook's questioning look.

'Yeah, the tracks lead straight into the badlands right enough.'

Carbrook sighed. He didn't like the idea of leading a weary posse out there into that no-man's-land of arroyos, cactus, twisted trails and little water, but he had no choice.

'OK, boys,' he said heavily. 'Let's fill leather.'

The men moved slowly. Knees were thick now with fatigue and there was a clamminess of dank sweat in their shirts that their bodies no longer warmed. The night was chilly and slender mist tatters wove above the prairie girth-high and gathered in the hollows. The men were bushed and the night was cold and getting colder, yet to a man they mounted up without protest. The discovery of Olan Fletcher's bullet-ridden corpse some time back had acted as a spur to flagging spirits. They were tired and cranky, but they were still ready to ride on.

All except one. 'I don't figger they're in the badlands,' opined Surprising Smith, making no attempt to mount.

He pointed north across the river. 'I've got a hunch they're over there.'

'How in the world do you figure that?' Carbrook wanted to know.

'Only a fool would ride into the badlands at night with three men to two horses, and a posse on his heels,' the bounty-hunter reasoned. 'And I don't reckon Sprod's any fool.'

'But the tracks lead in there.'

'Sure they do. But you know what I'd do if I was Sprod, Carbrook? I'd lay a false trail into the badlands, hopin' we'd follow it, then I'd put my horses to the river and ride back up this away and take off across that there easier country north.'

'A theory,' Carbrook said shortly. 'We don't have the time or energy for theories, Mr Smith. Come on, mount up.'

Surprising Smith shook his head. He was quite sure his theory was sound. He wanted Carbrook to lead the posse across on the north side of the Arrowhead and look for the outlaws' sign. Carbrook refused. An argument developed and finally Smith snapped.

'All right, you go your way and I'll go mine, Carbrook, and we'll see who's right.'

Carbrook protested. He didn't fancy the idea of going on into the badlands without Smith. Then, sensing Smith was challenging his authority, he began to realize he didn't really need Smith. Somewhere along the trail from Daybreak, the men riding with Carbrook had developed a unity and a sense of purpose he'd never have thought possible. If the bounty-hunter was so damned insistent on pulling out, then Carbrook felt that his men with their newfound strength of purpose could prove more than a match for Sprod when the showdown came.

Yet even so, he made one last attempt to get Smith to change his mind by threatening that he wouldn't get paid if he pulled out. Smith countered by declaring that if he didn't find Sprod, he got no bounty anyway. There were several more minutes of wrangling and testiness and then, fearing that his men might run out of steam with too long a delay, Carbrook bade his rebellious gunman and sign reader goodnight, and led the posse west.

Delaying only long enough to water his horse,

Surprising Smith forded the Arrowhead and cut west with his eyes on the ground.

By the time he'd gone a mile, the posse was out of sight, clattering along on Sprod's trail. Smith was as certain as he could be that Carbrook was wrong and he was right, yet the main reason the bounty-hunter had turned stubborn was that he wanted to get back to Daybreak as quickly as possible. He knew only too well what a hot little flirt his wife was, and all day long he'd been troubled by jealous thoughts of Honey and a certain good-looking gambler. No, he didn't feel he had time to waste poking about the badlands. The quicker he flushed Sprod the better – and such was the little man's vanity that he was confident he could take care of the fugitives alone when he did catch up with them.

Picking up the sign where the outlaw trio had left the Arrowhead just as he'd hazarded, the bounty-hunter tracked them north for several miles to Cripple Canyon and the old tumbledown ranch house of the Star 40. Sighting the two blown horses and a dim light in the old house, Surprising Smith staked down his horse and closed in silently, gun in fist, ready to add immeasurably to his fame by capturing or killing the three members of the Sprod bunch single-handed.

Perhaps he might have done just that if Sprod hadn't posted Frank Piano back trail to make certain that the posse followed his red herring trail. It was Piano who sighted the small solitary figure of Surprising Smith thirty minutes back, which was more than enough time for them to stake out the house and wait for him to come in.

Sprod knew his bad run of luck was continuing when,

with Smith about to drop into their laps like a ripe plum, Dick Grid got anxious and shot too soon.

The shot missed and Surprising Smith jumped like a startled antelope and, finding himself in open country with not a blade of grass to hide behind, had no alternative but to dash for the nearest outbuilding, a tumbledown barn. From there, as he blasted back at the outlaws with deadly accuracy, he quickly found himself encircled and the timbers of the old barn shuddering and crumbling about him under the chop of the angry lead.

The guns yammered to and fro like the voices of savage dogs. For Surprising Smith there was no way out, but the lethal accuracy of his lead kept the outlaws from closing in.

Stalemate.

And as the battle raged, the moon climbed high in the sky, the cold wind fell and the crashing thunder of the guns carried far on the still night air, all the way to Bighorn Ranch to the north . . . and all the way to the moon washed badlands to the south. . . .

ELEVEN

BIG FRIDAY

Hannibal Moore went along because he was the Reverend Martin's brother-in-law and because the Reverend hinted that Hannibal might be forced to quit sponging off him in the future if he didn't join them.

Thad Darcy joined in because he and Hannibal were drinking friends, while Tom Whitney went along just for the hell of it. Donny Dunn joined in because he hated Belle's girls who turned down his custom regularly every week on account he stank like a polecat. Slim Carter went with Donny because he liked the idea of running with a bunch, while Joe Parker simply went in the hope of being able to steal something if violence erupted down on the corner of Johnny and Piute.

Coming along in ones and twos to the Carbrook house which had been designated as the marshalling point for the 'march of protest' against Belle Shilleen's bordello, the recruits were surprised to find another dozen men already there, smoking cigarettes and looking a mite self-conscious about the whole thing. They shouldn't have been surprised for, to a man, those already there were husbands of the militant ladies of CLOD and the CLOD ladies were adept at nothing if it wasn't bossing their menfolk around. Joe and Mick and Sam were there because they didn't dare not to be. Besides, it might be fun.

By ten o'clock the crowd had grown to well over forty, roughly half men and half women. Mrs Carbrook was elated, but insisted on waiting a further fifteen minutes in case of late comers. The delay paid off when a dozen or more town loafers saw what was going on at the Carbrooks' and decided to join in the fun. The excitement in the air increased when Mrs Carbrook addressed them before they set out and emotion was already high by the time she had finished. One or two good customers of Belle Shilleen's were even heard to declare that maybe that great big red brick bordello was a bit much anyway.

The plan was to march on the bordello, show themselves and let the 'enemy' realize what they were up against. It was to be hoped then that Belle would throw in the towel and vacate the premises, after which they would be set alight. Bob Dunbar of the Kansas Insurance Company had revealed that the new building and its interior had been fully insured by Belle Shilleen. Therefore nobody would be caused any great hardship by what must be done, while at the same time a great blow would be struck for decency in Daybreak.

That was the plan. But so much for the best laid plans of mice and men. Everything went all right up to the point where Belle Shilleen was supposed to quit. But Belle didn't want to quit. Instead she got angry, pulled Matilda Carbrook's nose, and told them all to get to hell and gone away from her place before she *really* lost her temper.

That was when Donny Dunn got carried away and threw a brick through a window. Big 6 cowboy Brunk Carter immediately retaliated by striding out and knocking Donny flat with as good a right cross as had been seen in Daybreak for many a day.

Up until then there had been no real harm done. The mob, swelling by the minute now as others came down to see what was going on, milled around shouting at the house, not quite sure what they should do next or what direction proceedings should take. Inside, Belle Shilleen was good and mad about her broken window but still not taking things too seriously. Some of the girls who'd come from tough backgrounds were in favor of marching out and driving the mob off with whatever was handy, but were dissuaded by Belle's cowboy and towner clientele who still regarded the whole thing as a big joke.

Watching proceedings from the upstairs gallery in the company of Gypsy, Floralee, Mexican Rita and Benedict, Hank Brazos thought it a great joke too, and couldn't understand why Benedict was looking so pensive as he watched the carryings-on below.

'Seems to me you might have lost a lot of ginger since Pea Ridge, Yank,' he joshed good-humouredly. 'Seems to me it would have taken more than a bunch of old biddies to start you in bitin' your nails back there.'

Benedict didn't bother to answer, just went on

smoking his fine cigar with a small frown etching his brows. He didn't even smile when fat Mrs Jesse Morgan stumbled over a piece of lumber left over by the builders and sat down heavily, to wild applause. Benedict didn't like mobs. In his adventurous years in the West he'd seen too often what could happen when they got out of hand.

But if Duke Benedict was concerned, nobody else really was – until the gun went off. It was Tom Whitney's gun and Tom, getting carried away by the excitement of the occasion, decided it was time to liven things up a little and punched a shot harmlessly at the sky.

Inside the parlor, Big 6 cowboy Lee Hunter, drunk as could be, even when he'd arrived at Belle's, heard the shot, jumped to the wrong conclusion, and before anybody could stop him, hauled his gun and cut loose through the broken window.

Brazos and Benedict were diving for the stairs as Thad Darcy crumpled in the crowd with a bullet in the shoulder. By the time they stormed into the parlor, Hunter's friends had already taken care of him and he was spread out on the Brussels carpet with a lump the size of a pigeon's egg rising on his forehead.

'What a crazy thing to do,' Brazos said angrily. 'C'mon, Yank, we better go outside and quieten 'em down afore anybody else gets hurt.'

They only got as far as the door. The mob was advancing toting staves and lumber and bricks and anything they could lay hands on. In as long as it had taken Brazos and Benedict to get from the upper balcony to the front door, the thing that Benedict had feared had happened. The germ of hidden violence that nobody besides himself had really suspected was there at all, had in the matter of moments suddenly erupted into life. Suddenly this just wasn't a great big caper any more. Guns had been fired and Thad Darcy's blood was spilled there where they all could see it. Something unquenchable had arisen out of the earth, the boards, the very air of Daybreak itself. The beast of violence had been set loose. It showed in the eager wet-lipped face of the man who threw a brick, it was there in the flushed red faces, the women yelling at them to burn the bordello to the ground. It was there everywhere in faces grown suddenly cruel, in clutching hands and wet lips. It was the face of the mob, one of the ugliest sights on earth.

Benedict and Brazos just had time to leap back and slam the big front door before they hit it. The bordello shook with the impact. A Big 6 cowboy cleared his gun as a brick came whistling through the window and hit Baby Betty on the shin. Brazos reached the man with two strides, struck the gun aside. Wild-eyed, the cowpoke lashed out. Brazos chopped to the jaw with a punch that travelled no more than six inches and the man went down like a dead-fall log. There was a stutter of boot heels out back. The towner customers had decided it was time to quit.

'Douse the lights and take positions around the windows and doors!' Duke Benedict shouted above the tumult. 'The most important thing is to keep them out! Come on, get moving!'

The Big 6 men, wondering how the hell a night's fun had taken this turn, nevertheless obeyed with enthusiasm. They were wild boys who dearly loved a good ruckus, and defending a sporting house against a bunch of Bible-toting do-gooders somehow appealed to them.

Belle Shilleen and her girls were just as enthusiastic, and in those first hectic minutes of the attack, more attackers were driven off from their attempts to force their way through windows and doors by baton wielding girls in flimsy house costumes than by cowpunchers swinging their gun barrels.

But as that first attack intensified, with every ground level window and door under attack, it was Benedict and Brazos who bore the brunt of the mob's fury. Speeding from one danger point to another through the darkened house, they wielded their six-gun barrels with deadly effectiveness wherever a head appeared through a window, or some burly towner tried to force himself through a doorway, and it was mainly their rock-like defense that finally took the sting out of that first attack.

Belle Shilleen's girls broke into a triumphant cheer when the attack eased off, then ceased altogether. The mob re-formed out front, milled about a while, then went surging up Johnny Street towards the Carbrook house. But the cheers were premature. The attackers weren't quitting, just retiring to get their breath, to fire their enthusiasm with a little liquid courage, listen to a few rabble-rousing speeches, then get ready to strike again.

Duke Benedict sensed this even if the girls didn't, and as soon as the crowd had gone, he called Belle and Brazos upstairs for a confab. Belle had figured they'd carried the day and it was difficult to convince her the danger wasn't over. Brazos however agreed with Benedict and together they considered the situation as it stood.

There was obviously no point in trying to appeal to the mob; they were running hog wild. Sam Fink was out; he couldn't stop a dust-up between a bunch of toddle-age kids. There was no chance of Belle quitting and neither man wanted her to, but if the next attack turned really dangerous, they might have to start shooting, and they wanted to avoid that at all costs. They wanted the towners stopped, not killed. But who could do it? Was there a solution? There might be . . . and it was Benedict who finally came up with it.

The posse.

'By Judas, that's it!' applauded Brazos. 'Carbrook and the rest would put the lid on this in no time flat.' Then his face fell. 'But hell, we're gettin' ahead of ourselves a bit, ain't we, Yank? The posse's out to hell and gone doggin' Sprod someplace.'

Benedict had already considered that. 'Maybe they are,' he conceded. 'But they've been gone a long time, Reb, longer than anybody figured. They should be on their way home now, only stands to reason.'

'Mebbe it does at that. But how—?'

'One of us will have to go look for Carbrook, while the other stays here to stand by Belle,' Benedict decided. 'Maybe you'd better go and me stay, Reb. You'd likely make a better fist of tracking the posse down.'

'Do you really think it's that serious that you have to go looking for the posse?' Belle Shilleen said, worried now.

'I do, Belle,' replied Benedict. 'How about you, Reb?'

'Reckon so,' agreed Brazos. 'That there mob's got the wolf-pack feel now and they find they like it.'

'Oh all right,' the woman agreed. Then looking at

them both in turn, 'I won't forget all you've done for me tonight. I'm sure I don't know how I can repay you.'

Benedict had a good notion, but wasn't about to divulge it yet. 'All right, Reb,' he said quietly. 'You'd better get going.'

Brazos got going. Quitting the bordello, he took to a back street and headed for the central block. Passing the Carbrook house, he caught sight of the mob milling about in the backyard shouting and drinking and boasting what they were going to do in the next attack. The sight was ugly and a little chilling and spurred Brazos on just that much faster.

He'd better find that posse, and find it quick.

Brazos loped into Johnny Street a block beyond the Carbrook house and found the main stem deserted. Everybody was either with the mob or else locked indoors and waiting for Daybreak's storm of violence to burn itself out.

Brazos' lips twisted with contempt when he saw the light still burning in the jailhouse. The whole damned town could be burning down and that undersized little badge-packer wouldn't lift a finger. But maybe the deputy had some idea where the posse might be he guessed, and, heading for the livery to saddle up, he decided to call and see Fink before he headed out.

It proved to be the luckiest decision he could have made, for he found Fink all in a twitch. Two cowhands from the Big Horn Ranch five miles south of town had ridden in a short time back with the news that there was a gun battle going on at the old Star 40 Ranch in Cripple

Canyon. The hands figured it might be the posse come to grips with Ben Sprod and his bunch.

So did Brazos.

He left town at a dead run, highballing south. A few miles out, he reined in briefly and heard the distant sound of the guns. He spurred on, and fifteen minutes later reined in atop the north rim of Cripple Canyon close to the Star 40 ranch house where wicked red flashes of six-guns were flickering like deadly fireflies in the night.

Caching his horse, he headed swiftly towards the ranch house afoot, keeping to the deep moon shadows that were flung wide across the canyon floor by the towering walls.

The shadows played out two hundred yards from the old house, but well before reaching that spot he'd realized that this wasn't the posse doing battle with the Sprod bunch as he'd hoped, but what seemed like a solitary pilgrim holed up in an old barn having it out with two or three guns circled around him.

Right then, one of the outlaws leapt from the cover of a tree some fifty yards from the old barn and sprinted on long legs for the closer cover of a stack of old fence ties. The man was only visible for a matter of seconds, yet by the light of the brilliant moon, Brazos saw him just as clearly as he'd seen him yesterday morning when the lead had flown thick and hot around Morgan's Rock.

An unholy smile creased Hank Brazos' face then as he poked his hat back from his forehead with the barrel of his six-gun and breathed, 'Well, I'll be dogged! Sprod!'

A moment later he was snaking forward and counting on speed and surprise to get him up there before they spotted him.

TWELVE

BATTLE OF CRIPPLE CANYON

Surprising Smith stroked the trigger and the six-gun bucked against the crotch of his hand. For a moment the stack of fence ties was obscured in smoke, but even before Sprod's Colt started to snarl back from that position, Smith knew he'd missed.

They were closing in. There was no doubt about that now. For hours he'd been able to keep them at a distance with his pinpoint marksmanship, but he was running desperately low on slugs now and they knew it. The wolves could smell the blood of the kill.

Surprising Smith wasn't all that surprised to realize that he wasn't afraid of dying. Fear had never been one of his drawbacks. All that really bothered him was uncertainty about whether his little wife would suitably mourn his passing. Honey was nothing if not flirtatious, and you could bet that tinhorn gambling man would be around to comfort her in her tragic bereavement. . . .

Smith's thoughts were shattered as a slug ricocheted off a foundation stone and bit into his calf. The shot had come from behind the ruin of an old overturned buckboard less than thirty yards west of the barn. The little gunman smiled a cold smile. Throughout the long hours of the siege, he'd been hoping somebody would mistake weather-rotted old boards for sound cover.

He took his time aiming, resting his gun hand on a fallen crossbeam. The flare of the shot had come from the left end of the buckboard. He moved his sights two feet in from the edge, held the six-gun rock steady, then let loose three shots in one continuous, rolling roar.

The bullets ripped through the timbers of the old buckboard like they were paper. One caught Dick Grid in the chest, another in the throat, a third in the head. The combined impact flung the badman six feet back, dead three times over without so much as a scream. Standing behind the tie stack, Ben Sprod ground his teeth in fury as Grid's beefy corpse rolled out underneath the moon. Sprod then cut loose with a furious volley. Surprising Smith's gun churned back twice and then clearly Sprod heard the sound of a hammer clicking on an empty chamber.

Hope glittering in his eyes, Sprod loosed three shots, then waited. No response. He fired again, emptying his gun. Swiftly reloading, he peered around the corner of the stack at the tumbledown barn. Had the bounty-hunter finally run out of bullets? He had to be damned close to it, Sprod figured, considering all the powder he'd burned over the past couple of hours keeping the three of them at bay.

A minute passed. Two . . . and still no shots from the barn.

Sprod cupped a hand to his mouth. 'Frank!' he shouted across to the crouched figure behind the old stone well on the south-east side of the barn. 'He's out of slugs! Close in!'

Frank Piano didn't think that was such a hell of a good idea and said so, but quickly his mind changed when a slug from Sprod slashed the earth a foot behind his boots.

'I said we're closin' in,' Sprod yelled. 'Get goin'!'

Frank Piano rose warily and moved slowly towards the barn in a low crouch, ready to hurl himself back behind the well if Surprising Smith turned out to be just playing possum. Moonlight sheened on his pale, tense face as he shot a glance across at the tie stack to see if Ben was coming with him, but Ben was staying put. No sense in them both being caught out in the open if things went sour, was the way Sprod reasoned.

Frank Piano covered another tense ten paces. In the old barn, Surprising Smith watched him come and felt cold sweat run down his face. He only had two slugs left. He had to make dead certain of getting the bandy-legged badman with one and having one left for Sprod.

It was eerily still in Cripple Canyon, even the night birds and foraging animals seeming to fall still, waiting for the guns to erupt again. No breath of wind stirred, no blade of grass whispered, just the dusty creak of Frank Piano's boots, and the tight sound of his breathing as he drew to within twenty yards of his objective, then fifteen. . . .

And in that electric silence, the sudden sound of the big voice from behind Sprod sounded like so many gun-shots.

'Drop your guns, outlaws!'

Ben Sprod spun about, sunken eyes twin points of total disbelief in the lizard head. His jaw fell open but no sound came out as he stared at the wide-shouldered figure in the purple shirt, with the gun in his big fist that looked the size of a cannon.

'I said drop 'em, outlaw,' Brazos' voice was cartridge clear. 'Drop 'em or use 'em!'

Ben Sprod tried to use them and Brazos' gun spewed fire. Bullets tore into Ben Sprod with sledge-hammer force, smashing him back into the tie stack. White-hot pain ripped through him as the gun went on firing, flooding through every part of his body as he fell and darkness and oblivion reached out and drew him in.

Brazos flung himself low as shots sounded from the barn. But they weren't meant for him. With Surprising Smith's last two bullets in him, Frank Piano fell, twitched and threshed hideously on the ground for ten seconds that seemed like a full minute, then snapped taut, and died.

Brazos rose, and fingered fresh shells into his hot gun. 'Howdy-do,' he said amiably as Surprising Smith picked his way out of the ruins with his empty six-gun pointing to the ground. 'You OK, mister?'

Surprising Smith walked up, looked at Ben Sprod for a moment then spat on him. Then he nodded, 'Yeah, I'm all right, just fresh out of shells, is all.'

Brazos waited for more, but there wasn't any more. The little black-garbed bounty-hunter hunkered silently down beside Sprod's corpse and calmly filled his gun from the outlaw's shell belt and Brazos wondered if maybe the surprising thing about Surprising Smith was that he didn't seem to have an ounce of gratitude in his runty little body.

His voice was gruff and short-tempered as he gave the bounty-hunter a brief rundown of what had happened in town and how he came to be out here.

Then he said, 'You got any idea where I'll find the posse now?'

Smith knew exactly where the posse was, but doubted if they'd be able to track it down in the badlands. Brazos said they'd just have to damn well try, and they went and fetched their horses and struck south.

Hank Brazos was in a sour mood as they left Cripple Canyon behind. If Surprising Smith was aware of the other's mood he gave no sign but just sat his saddle smoking a cigarette and watching the way ahead. It didn't make Brazos warm to him any when, just a few minutes after leaving the canyon, Smith was the first to see the plume of dust rising from the trail just a short distance ahead.

The flower vase was made of solid brass and weighed about ten pounds. Floralee was breathing heavily as she struggled to lift it to perch precariously on the railing of the upper gallery, but she made it, and grunted with satisfaction as she gave Benedict a 'you watch this' look.

Moments later Hannibal Moore's baldy skull appeared in the moonlight below. Moore, with a half-dozen others had been busily engaged for the past ten minutes in trying unsuccessfully to batter down the front door with a fence post.

The vase dropped dead on target and made contact with Hannibal's skull with a noise like a Chinese gong. Angry shouts rose from below followed by a fusillade of stones that drove Benedict and the girl inside.

Floralee giggled as she scouted around to see if she could find another vase. 'Ain't this good, Duke? I swear I haven't had so much fun since I don't know when.'

Without response, Benedict headed down the stairs. This was another of those times when he saw himself objectively and with distaste. Duke Benedict, college graduate, ex-army officer and man of distinction, now in command of the defenses of a hick-town house of ill-fame under siege by a bunch of women and pot-bellied towners. How in hell had he gotten himself into a situation like this? Glimpsing Belle Shilleen as she patched up a Big 6 cowboy's cracked head he immediately knew why. If he hadn't stayed by Belle tonight, then he wouldn't have a prayer in hell of her telling him anything about Bo Rangle. No, he mused, he didn't have any choice. But by the tarnal, if Belle *did* tell him what he wanted to know, he'd have earned it.

The gambler's nose wrinkled in disgust as he entered the parlor. It looked, for want of a better word, like a brothel. With eyes that had grown accustomed to the semi-darkness, he glimpsed smashed furniture, a carpet of broken glass, a clutch of battered cowpunchers standing guard at the windows and keeping themselves fortified with whisky from Belle's bar. Baby Betty, Darling Jill and Kitty Kellick were wearily picking up the bricks that had been thrown in and throwing them back out at the mob. Belle was bandaging Jimmy Dolan who'd been hit with a flying bottle while, miraculously it seemed, the steam piano had so far avoided serious damage. The room stank of whisky, smoke and sweaty bodies and by the sound of it the mob was building up a fresh attack out back. No, this wasn't Duke Benedict's finest hour, by a country mile.

Belle finished with Jimmy Dolan and came across to him with her impressive undulating walk that remained unaffected by adversity. She chucked him under the chin and grinned. 'Well, what news from the front, Captain?'

Benedict had to hand it to Belle. She was made of tough stuff. She came from Alabama, and he had a sneaking suspicion that if Robert E. Lee had tapped the South's womanhood for his armies, then the result of the War of the States just might have been somewhat different.

'No sign of Brazos yet,' he growled, then whipped around at a squeal from the window. Two towners were making a determined bid to force their way in, and Gypsy was swatting at them with a steel-tipped walking cane.

Benedict drew both guns and made it across the room in three bad-tempered strides. He swung first with his right-hand gun, then with the left. Two solid thuds and the window was cleared again, with shouts of chagrin rising from outside.

'Oh, Duke, you're so strong and brave!' Gypsy cooed.

'Keep a sharp lookout,' was all Benedict said in response, then, holstering his guns, went back to Belle. 'I was just about to say,' he said as if there had been no interruption, 'that Brazos has been long gone. Doesn't look too hopeful I'm afraid.'

'He'll bring help,' Belle said cheerfully. 'I've got confidence in that boy.'

'I wish I had.'

'You have and you know it. And not only have you got confidence in him, Duke, you like him too, even if you go around sayin' you don't.'

Benedict snorted. 'It's hardly the time for character analysis, Belle. But you're wrong as could be. He's just a big dumb saddle tramp without enough brains to make his head ache.'

'Is that why you're joinin' up with him to look for that gold you're interested in?'

Benedict swore. 'He told you that?'

'Sure. During the party while you were showing us how you could play the piano.' She patted his hand. 'But don't be peeved, honey. It doesn't matter that I know.'

Maybe it didn't, but Benedict didn't like the idea of Belle and Hank Brazos getting their heads together.

He said carefully, 'About Bo Rangle—'

'Later, honey,' she cut in. 'I appreciate if it wasn't for you and Hank I'd be sittin' outside watchin' them burn my house to the ground by now.' She smiled in the gloom. 'Sure I'll help you, Duke. When it's time.'

Again they were interrupted by fresh sounds of violence, this time from the rear of the house. Hurrying out and along the corridor together, they found Mexican

Rita lying stunned on the floor from a brick and none other than Mrs Carbrook herself thrusting through the window with a burning brand, trying to set the drapes alight.

'This one's mine,' Belle said grimly and spitting on her hands and striding forward she reefed the blazing brand out of the woman's hand, reversed it and jabbed it at her face. She was only feinting, but Matilda Carbrook didn't know that. She squawked in terror, fell to the ground, then struggled to her feet and staggered out of harm's way screaming that that scarlet woman had tried to set her on fire, her cries drawing cries of 'shame' from the mob.

Then suddenly, even as Belle watched, the volume of shouting began to die down and their faces turned away from the house. She saw a man gesticulate towards the road, then caught a glimpse of Matilda Carbrook standing there with her big fat face hanging open in astonishment. What on earth was going on?

She spun on her heel as Benedict shouted excitedly from the window at the far end of the corridor. 'Belle, come here quick!'

Gathering up her skirts she ran the length of the hallway, reached Benedict's side and looked out. Her heart skipped a full beat and tears of relief burst from her eyes.

Reining in at the hitch rack out front in his bright purple shirt, was Hank Brazos. And the posse was behind him.

For a mob that just minutes ago had been making more noise that night than Daybreak had ever heard before, the hundred and fifty citizens that comprised that crowd were astonishingly subdued as Mayor Humphrey Carbrook swung down from his saddle, tugged ominously at the lapels of his old-fashioned frock coat and made a bee-line directly for his wife.

Or was that his wife? Surely this fat, uncertain little woman wasn't the same blustering Matilda Carbrook who had led them all down here and given them the catch-cry that had shaken Daybreak from end to end a hundred times over the past hours: 'Burn the Bordello. Burn the Bordello!'

Yes it was, but it wasn't a Matilda Carbrook that Daybreak knew. Nobody would have believed that Matilda Carbrook could look so guilty.

'Now, Humphrey,' she stammered, trying to muster some of the old authority as he came to a grim-jawed halt before her. 'Before you lose your temper, I insist—'

'Matilda Carbrook, get yourself home immediately!'

Matilda quivered in the full blast of husbandly wrath. She felt a little frightened, but also a little thrilled; she'd never known Humphrey quite so dominating.

Even so, she felt she must try and save some face, as she made an attempt to draw herself up with some dignity. 'Humphrey, I warned you before you left on that ridiculous posse that—'

'That "ridiculous posse" as you so term it, Matilda,' her masterful husband overrode her, 'has been instrumental in ridding this country once and for all of the Scourge of Calico Valley!'

This was the first intimation that the crowd had had of Sprod's death. Up until that moment, they, like Matilda

Carbrook herself, had been somewhat caught on the wrong leg by the return of the posse, but they still had some ideas about carrying on with what they'd begun. But this news was something immeasurably bigger and more important than any brick bordello.

'You mean Ben Sprod's done for, Mayor Carbrook?' a man in the crowd called wonderingly.

'Done for,' Carbrook confirmed. 'Along with Frank Piano and Dick Grid. The three of them were gunned down by Hank Brazos and Surprising Smith not an hour ago in Cripple Canyon.'

A mighty cheer went up, hats sailed in the air and carried away by the news, Harp Moody filled his lungs and bellowed:

'Free drinks at the Bird Cage, boys. If this don't call for a celebration I don't know what does!'

'Stop!' Matilda Carbrook cried as they started to stream away 'Stop I say! What about this house of sin?' Nobody heeded her, except her husband. Wearing the long-suffering look of a man who has finally run completely out of patience, Humphrey Carbrook seized his wife in a powerful grip, sat himself down on the fence and proceeded to paddle her ample bottom.

A dozen solid whacks later, he sat her back on her feet and struck a pose, hands on hips. 'Well, Matilda?'

The posse men and the watchers from the house waited expectantly for the explosion. None came. Matilda Carbrook had just received what she'd badly needed for fifty years and felt a better woman for it. 'I'm sorry, Humphrey,' she said meekly. 'I really am.'

'And so you should be. Now, on your way home, that is

of course after you've apologized to Belle for the trouble you've caused. . .'

Matilda looked across at the house where Belle Shilleen, Duke Benedict and the others had come out onto the flame-scarred porch. Then she looked back at her husband who was frowning mightily. She sighed and went across to the gallery.

'I'm very sorry, Miss Shilleen. Can you forgive me?'

'I suppose so,' Belle replied stiffly. Then relaxing, 'Sure, why not? Only don't try nothin' like this again, will you, kid? I might have to take it personal next time.'

'Oh no, no,' Matilda said hastily. 'I give you my word. I realize now I was very foolish.' She turned and looked adoringly at her husband. 'Humphrey made me realize that. Are you going to walk me home, Humphrey?'

Humphrey Carbrook bowed courteously, extended his arm. 'Thank you, gentlemen,' he said to his posse men, 'and in particular, thank you, Mr Brazos and Mr Smith. Come along, my dear.'

They went off arm in arm down the street and the posse started to break up. Brazos dismounted, tethered his horse to the tie-rack and ambled through the gateway 'Well, some openin' night, eh, folks?' he grinned.

'Oh, Hank, you wonderful man,' Gypsy cried, rushing out to throw her arms about him, almost knocking him off his feet. 'We knew you'd make it, we just knew!'

'Yeah, well I just about didn't,' Brazos drawled. 'Not in time that is,' he added, then went on to tell them how he and Surprising Smith had caught up with the posse south of Cripple Canyon after the shootout with the Sprod bunch. The posse had heard the gunfire, and guessing

Smith had flushed the outlaws, had headed north for the canyon but had been delayed a dozen times by the rugged terrain of the badlands. 'Seems as well we bumped into 'em when we did,' Brazos concluded, eyes going over the scene of battle. 'By the looks of it you wouldn't have held out too much longer.'

'Well I mightn't have held out much longer myself,' grinned Benedict, able to joke about it now, 'but I'm damned if I think the girls would have quit.' He looked around at the girls gathered about him. 'I think now is the appropriate time to commend each and every one of you young ladies for your courage. You did yourselves proud.'

'Oh, don't he talk lovely though,' Floralee sighed.

'He certainly does,' Belle Shilleen said affectionately, slipping her arm around the gambler's waist. 'And never mind about you thankin' us, Duke, it's we should thank you – you and Hank.'

'My pleasure, Belle,' Brazos replied gracefully.

'Well, are we goin' to just stand around all night being polite?' Gypsy wanted to know. 'Or we goin' to start cleanin' house?'

'The house-cleanin' can wait,' declared Belle Shilleen. 'This is still Friday night, and Friday night's openin' night for Belle Shilleen's new house and by golly we're goin' to have ourselves our openin' night party regardless.' Everybody thought Belle was crazy at first. Yet it was astonishing how better things looked when they got the lamps lit again, straightened up the furniture and swept the glass from the main parlor. Little Bob French, who'd spent the entire period of the siege crouched down behind his bar, bobbed up and started serving drinks again with a will, while Benedict got the steam piano playing once again. The girls cleaned up hurriedly, put on fresh, pretty gear and started dancing – for the second time that night – with the Big 6 cowboys.

Ten minutes later a couple of the posse men wandered in and joined the fun. The piano built up a head of steam and the music carried all the way down Johnny Street and the word went swiftly around that there was open house at Belle Shilleen's. Within thirty minutes the place was packed. Harp Moody closed the Bird Cage and came down with his wife and his percentage girls and a load of free liquor. The Reverend Martin arrived with his wife, to apologize to Belle for their part in what had happened earlier, and stayed on to demonstrate to all and sundry the new dance step they'd learned in Denver while on vacation.

It was without question the greatest party in Daybreak's history. The Ben Sprod bunch was finished, and the attack on the bordello earlier had somehow brought all the meanness of the town to the surface, then got rid of it. People who hadn't spoken to one another for years, drank together with their arms about each other. Matilda Carbrook arrived with a huge cake and was promptly whisked off to dance with Henry Peck who'd never been known to dance a step in his life. Music, dancing, pretty women, gaiety, and a feeling that they were burying old times and beginning afresh. What more could a party want to make it truly memorable?

Nothing, one would have guessed. Yet at dawn the thing happened that would positively guarantee against anybody ever forgetting the great night of the party at Belle Shilleen's. That was when Surprising Smith showed up in his neat black shirt and his tight black pants and his low-crowned black hat to challenge Duke Benedict to a duel to the death.

THIRTEEN

VERY SURPRISING

Benedict came out of the bordello with the revelers filling the doors and windows behind him. The gambling man had thought Flash Jimmy Chadwick might be putting him on when he told him Surprising Smith was waiting for him out front. But Smith was there right enough, a dark, neat little figure on the plank walk, silhouetted against the dawn-washed gray of the street.

Benedict walked slowly out onto the walk followed by a babble of excited speculation. Some thought this must be part of the entertainment.

'So, at least you had the guts to come out,' was Surprising Smith's grating greeting. 'Well, just as well you did, tinhorn, on account I'd of come in after you right smart.'

'What's on your mind, Smith?' Benedict wanted to know. The gambler looked much bigger than the little bounty-hunter standing there with the chill early morning wind fluttering his black four-in-hand tie. He also looked far more formidable with his unbuttoned coat revealing the polished black gunbelt slanted across his hips and the big white-handled Colts. His teeth flashed in a grin that sent a flutter through the women in the watching crowd.

'Flash Jimmy told me as how you wanted to gunfight me, but of course I know he made a mistake.'

'I *am* here to gunfight you, tinhorn.'

'You must be loco. Why would we want to fight?'

'You know only too damned well, blast your eyes.' Smith's mouth twisted. 'You dirty wife-stealer!'

It was seldom that Duke Benedict was genuinely innocent where the pretty wives of irate husbands were concerned, but this was one of them. Innocent only perhaps because of a combination of bad luck and lack of opportunity, but innocent nonetheless.

'Now see here, Smith,' he protested, 'I haven't—'

'They told me up at the saloon that you been hangin' about her while I been gone,' the jealous little manhunter cut him off. 'I gave her a good larrupin', but she still wouldn't admit you seduced her. But I know her, and I know your smooth-talkin' tinhorn breed – and that's why I aim to put you in the ground.'

Benedict's face turned cold. 'You beat up on Honey?' Before Smith could reply, Hank Brazos loomed up behind Benedict.

'What's eatin' you, Smith?' the big man demanded. 'You likkered up?'

'Better stay out of this, Reb,' Benedict said.

'Yeah,' Surprising Smith agreed. 'I got no beef with

you, Brazos, just your fancy-fingered, high-rollin' friend.'

'Now just a dad-blamed minute—'

'Back off, Brazos,' Benedict commanded. 'This is my card game.'

Brazos grumbled and moved back. Benedict turned back to Smith, making one last effort to avoid gunsmoke. 'Now look, Smith, can't we talk this over?'

'Go for your irons you philanderin', wife-stealin' son-of-a-bitch!'

Those harsh words brought a sudden hush to the crowd that watched, as motley and colorful a crowd as Calico Valley had ever seen. They were lining both galleries of Belle's house now, hanging out of windows and doors for a better view and with a score or more grouped about in the littered front yard.

'All right, bounty-hunter,' Benedict said coldly, flipping the panels of his coat back behind his gun butts. 'If you're bound and determined to die a fool . . . draw!'

Surprising Smith delayed just a moment to get himself set, and in that moment, each man became aware of the rapid pitter-patter of high heels on the boardwalk. Other heads turned to see Honey Smith running down the street with her long black hair flying behind her, but not Benedict or Smith. Their eyes were locked on each other, they were as still as death.

And then they drew.

Flashing hands drove downwards, and as he came clear, Benedict noted with ice-cold professional interest that Surprising Smith was surprisingly fast. But as skilled hands slapped bone and thornwood grips, and the deadly guns leapt, a piercing cry broke the electric hush.

'Cedric! Cedric, no!'

The voice registered with Benedict, but not the name Cedric. But both registered with Surprising 'Cedric' Smith, and for a split-second the little bounty-hunter's concentration was affected by his wife's voice, robbing him of that razor edge of speed that could mean the difference between life and death.

It would have been death, if Duke Benedict were a killer. But the gambler didn't really want to kill this cranky little gamecock, and the bullet that snarled from his right hand Colt didn't rip through the bounty-hunter's heart as it might have, but through his right hand, sending his six-gun spinning into the dust.

A great sigh of relief came from the watching crowd as Duke Benedict lowered his smoking gun. Surprising Smith gasping, clutched at his bloody hand and turned to face his wife. Honey's hair was disheveled, she was sporting a black eye, but still looked pretty as a heart flush to Duke Benedict.

'Cedric Smith,' she stormed, disgusted, 'I warned you, didn't I? I warned you you'd be a fool if you didn't believe I'd been true to you, and a double fool if you called Duke out over it.'

She paused for breath, put her hands on her hips and regarded him sternly. 'Now just take a look at yourself, Cedric. You've gone and got yourself hurt, and you've made a fool of yourself and me in front of the whole town. Aren't you ashamed?'

Relieved, trying not to grin, Duke Benedict waited for Honey's words to strike sparks off Surprising Smith's flinty temper. But Cedric Surprising Smith just stood there looking smaller and more foolish by the moment as his furious wife continued to chew him out. He took his medicine like any ordinary house-broken husband, and suddenly, almost in the same moment, Benedict and the crowd sensed the truth about the bounty-hunter. Surprising Smith's pride and courage had all hinged on one thing; his gun speed. Now he'd tasted defeat and injury, he was revealed for what he really was. A very little man. Surprisingly little in fact.

Chuckling as Honey's tirade continued, Hank Brazos ranged up at Benedict's shoulder.

'You know, right about now, Yank, ole Surprisin' is wonderin' if it wouldn't have been better if you'd got him right twixt the eyes instead of just wingin' him.'

Benedict smiled openly. Then feeling just a little sorry for Smith now, elected to intervene.

'I think he's got the idea he was a little hasty, now, Honey,' he said, stepping forward. Then to Smith, 'You're a good hand with a gun, er, Cedric. But you're not any world-beater. I would have beaten you whether your lady wife had distracted you or not. Take a tip from one who knows. . . learn a lesson and give up gun work before you cross trails with somebody faster than me.'

'Mebbe I will at that, Benedict.' Smith was humble as a saint.

'There is no maybe about it, Cedric Smith,' declared Honey, who was showing an assertiveness new both to Benedict and her husband. 'I've had more than enough of this ridiculous way of life we lead. We're taking the first stage back home to Dog Hollow and I'll open up my dress shop again and you'll return to your rightful trade as a pastry cook.'

Deadly Surprising Smith the bounty-hunter, actually Cedric Smith, pastry cook from Dog Hollow? A titter ran through the crowd as they say in burlesque houses. The titter became open laughter when the ex-bounty-hunter just said meekly, 'All right, dear.'

'Well, at last you're showing some sense,' Honey sniffed, and watching her, Duke Benedict had a vision of Honey in ten years' time, thirty pounds heavier and bossy as a trainload of Irish railroad foremen. Poor Cedric, he remembered thinking, but put on his best smile as Honey ran to him with a softened expression.

'Thanks, Duke. I'll never forget you spared my Cedric's life.'

'My great pleasure,' Benedict murmured, giving a little bow. 'Au revoir, Honey. And goodbye to you, Cedric.'

Honey smiled farewell then as she took her husband by the arm. But there were no goodbye words from Surprising Smith, as he took one last woebegone look around the colorful scene under the rays of the rising sun, then like a weary little old man, let himself be led down Johnny Street, first to the hotel, then to the Stage Depot, and from there out of Daybreak, never to be seen or heard of in Calico Valley again.

'Now, Belle?'

'What's that, honey?'

'Are you ready to tell me where Rangle is now? I mean you promised you would if I stuck by you, and I did.'

'Sure, why not? You've earned it, honey.'

Benedict leant eagerly forward on the edge of the chaise lounge in Belle's upstairs room. It was an hour since the 'showdown' with Surprising Smith. The revelers had gone home and the officially-opened bordello was quiet.

Except for that furtive creak outside the door.

Benedict jumped up, strode to the door and flung it open. Hank Brazos stood there with an unlit cigarette dangling from his bottom lip.

'Howdy-do, Yank.'

'What the blue blazes are you doing listening at the door?' Benedict said angrily.

'Wasn't listenin', I was just about to knock,' Brazos said airily as he pushed past and leant lazily on the end of Belle's big brass bed. 'But I couldn't help overhearin' some,' he confessed. 'And seein' as how we're partners, Yank, why I don't see no harm in me sittin' in. Do you, Miss Belle?'

'Of course not,' Belle said, stretching luxuriously on the bed. Belle had changed into something more comfortable, a transparent creation which enabled Brazos to confirm his suspicion that Belle had one of the most generously-developed figures in the West.

Benedict went right on glowering silently at Brazos, but Belle didn't seem to notice.

'OK,' she said, 'Bo's got a hideout in the Maverick Hills just north of the town of Shoot across the border in Missouri. You could do worse than take a look there.'

'Thanks, Belle,' Brazos grinned and came around the side of the bed and kissed her cheek. 'And you can bet money that if I'm ever back in Calico Valley, I'll be callin' back to visit Belle Shilleen.'

'Oh, you're not leavin' right away?'

'Sorry, but I reckon so,' Brazos drawled, going to the door. 'Comin', Yank?'

'Huh? Oh yeah, yeah,' Benedict replied. He was annoyed that Brazos had found out what he'd hoped to learn alone, but there was nothing he could do about it now. Then, as Brazos had done, he crossed the bed and kissed the woman. 'Au revoir, Belle,' he murmured.

He made to turn away, but Belle had hold of his sleeve. 'Hey, just a minute, honey,' she said warmly, rubbing her cheek up against his hand and purring. 'You're not in that much of a hurry, surely, that you can't say goodbye to Belle properly.'

'Of course he ain't, Belle,' Brazos grinned from the door. 'When it comes to showin' off his manners and doin' the right thing, why, old Duke's got everybody I know licked holler.' He sketched a salute at the glaring Benedict as he went out. 'See you at the livery . . . partner.'

FOURTEEN

PARTNERS

Benedict was just getting dressed and buckling on his guns when Belle's door was kicked open without warning and he found himself looking down the barrel of a six-gun and above it, a face he hadn't seen since Pea Ridge, Georgia. . . .

Benedict's hand flashed to gun butt froze as Bo Rangle curled back the hammer of his hogleg and came striding in with a brace of dust-coated hardcases hard behind him.

'Don't stop, tinhorn,' Rangle grinned, though the smile didn't reach his eyes. 'Seems I ain't killed me a tinhorn all day.'

'Bo!' Belle Shilleen gasped from the bed, turning as white as chalk. 'Bo, how, what. . . ?'

Bo Rangle motioned to Dunstan to take Benedict's guns, then turned his frosty smile on the woman. 'Big surprise, Belle? Yeah, I guess it is.' The eyes flicked significantly at Benedict. 'Well, the truth is I just took it in my head to come along and take a look-see how openin' night went. When I strolled in downstairs and asked where you were, why the girls did get themselves into a twitch, tellin' me as how you were asleep and up the street, and gone back to visit your ma in Texas and Lordy knows what else. Right away I got me the stink of a skunk, didn't I, boys?'

'Bo, please,' Belle pleaded, and Benedict could see that she was afraid, not for herself as much as for him. 'Bo, it's not what you think. I was just—'

'Entertainin'?' Rangle said amiably. 'Sure, sure.' Then without a word of warning, lashed out with his six-gun. Benedict tried to duck. Too late. The barrel caught him across the forehead, knocking him back across Belle's side table.

For an agonized moment Benedict fought against the blinding pain, then pushed himself erect. Bo Rangle was only a blur, but Benedict saw his head nod. The next second Dunstan's iron fist smashed into his kidneys, followed by a punch from Skelley to the side of the head. . .

Benedict heard Belle scream as he lashed out. More blows rained down and a kick to the groin that sent a flame of agony pouring through him. He felt himself falling and heard Rangle's mocking voice.

'Never did come across a tinhorn with a lick of guts. They're good for nothin' but cheatin' with cards and shinin' up to women that don't belong to them.'

Rangle's boot caught Benedict in the guts, doubling him to the floor, but with a fierce burst of tiger-like energy he regained his feet and butted Rangle viciously in the middle. He had the small satisfaction of seeing Rangle stagger before the hard fists of Dunstan and Skelley smashed him down again. He felt the carpet against his face, heard a great roaring in his ears, a flash of fire, then oblivion.

It was the smelling salts that finally brought him around. His head jerked up and he found himself blinking up into the face of Floralee. The girl smiled and stroked his forehead.

'Now you just stay right there, Duke,' Floralee admonished him as he swung his feet off the sofa. 'You're one sick feller.'

Duke Benedict didn't need any hustler to tell him that. Thrusting the girl aside, he got to his feet, stood swaying for a moment, then lurched unsteadily across to the bar. Little Bob French didn't have to be told what was needed. Benedict downed his large bourbon at a gulp, and found he could focus on his reflection in the bar mirror. He looked like twenty miles of bad road and felt like it too, until he remembered what had happened and anger overrode the pain.

He swung to face the room. Belle's girls were all staring at him apprehensively. He spat blood and dabbed at his crimson lips. 'How did I get down here?' he demanded.

It was Gypsy who answered. 'They threw you downstairs after they beat you up, Duke. Oh, Duke, I'm so sorry we couldn't warn you that they were here. It just happened so suddenly. . . .'

Benedict tilted his head to the ceiling. 'Are they still up there?'

'Yes.'

'And Belle, is she all right?'

Gypsy looked anguished. 'I don't know, Duke. We just daren't go up. I've seen Bo mad before. He's . . . he's like an animal.'

'Not like one,' Benedict corrected, 'he *is* one.' With that he straightened from the bar and walked a little unsteadily through to the adjoining room. When he reappeared, he was toting two six-guns left over from the wild night.

The girls paled when they saw the guns. Gypsy moved quickly to block his way to the hall doorway.

'Duke, you're not goin' up there again?'

Benedict pushed Gypsy gently but firmly aside and went silently out into the passageway. As he reached the stairs he heard a door open and the sound of heavy feet in thc corridor above.

'The Madam ain't available!' Bo Rangle's wide mouth twisted as if the words scalded his mouth. 'You jokers ever hear that sayin'?'

Standing either side of the door, Skelley and Dunstan nodded vigorously. Sure they'd heard it. In some sporting houses they even had a printed sign to that effect.

'The Madam ain't available!' Rangle repeated, and his glare at Belle Shilleen was like a knife thrust.

'You were maybe expectin' me to wait forever until you took it into your head to drop me a line, Bo?' Belle replied firmly. A dark bruise was spreading down one side of her face where Rangle had struck her after they had thrown Benedict out, but she still showed plenty of nerve. If anything the beating she'd taken from Rangle had given her added strength. 'Why didn't I hear from you in all that time anyway?'

'Because I've been goddamn busy. I'm still goddamn busy only I made the big effort to get down here for openin' night. And what do I find? First I find some sort of a goddamn circus goin' on so I got to lay low half the goddamn night. Then there's a gunfight in the street, and when I finally mosey in with everything quiet, I find you two-timin' me with a tinhorn dude. Some home-comin'.' He snorted in disgust. 'Well I guess I cain't rightly bellyache. Like they always say, never trust a whore.'

The words were meant to cut and hurt but somehow they didn't. Studying her one-time lover gravely, Belle Shilleen was realizing just how much he'd changed in three months. She'd heard rumors that he'd been having it hard with a bunch in Missouri and she believed it now. Bo Rangle had always been a cruel and violent man yet not without a certain reckless charm. Now the charm was missing and the cruelty and the violence seemed to have taken over.

Rangle went on to give her some more bad tongue, until realizing he wasn't making much impression, he picked up his hat and jammed it on his head with an air of finality.

'All right, Belle,' he said flatly, 'so you've crossed me, so that's your right as a pathetic old whore I guess. But I'm afraid it's goin' to have to cost you, Belle. Now, what was our arrangement here, financially I mean?'

'Fifty-fifty.'

'Sounds a fair shake, wouldn't you say, boys?' Rangle enquired of his henchmen.

They nodded in unison and he went on. 'Yeah, sounds a fair shake to me. Maybe that's where I made a mistake . . . bein' too generous. Well all that's past as of now. It's now seventy-five percent for me, twenty-five percent for you . . . sweetheart.'

Belle Shilleen was too spent to protest. Two weary, it seemed, even to speak, she leant against the wall near her bed head, staring back at Bo Rangle with eyes that were almost as cold and hate-filled as his own.

Rangle understood that sort of emotion far better than he understood sentimentality or love. 'Seventy-five, twenty-five, Belle,' he repeated softly, then with a mocking gesture, turned and strode for the stair head, his henchmen hard behind. They had gone less than half a dozen steps when Glede Skelley suddenly seized Rangle by the arm and jabbed a finger. 'Hey, boss! Look, it's the dude.'

Rangle looked, but didn't see any dude. What he saw half-way up the stairs, was the head and shoulders of a hard-eyed pilgrim that bore a sketchy resemblance to the man they'd pounded into the floor and tossed downstairs a while back. Maybe it was the same man all right, but he sure didn't look like any dude with those two cannons in his fists.

The trio lunged for cover and Benedict cut loose. Rangle was his prime target, but Rangle got behind black-bearded Dunstan. Lead smashed through lips and teeth. Dunstan screamed then stopped screaming as lead punched his head askew and keyholed out his neck.

Searching lead burned furrows out of steps and stairway as Benedict flung himself to one side and sent a searching scythe of .45s churning through the gunsmoke. He missed Rangle, got a bead on Skelley. Skelley's gun hammered harmless lead into the ceiling as something punched him in the chest and iron blows broke him apart inside. Staring at his own blood curiously, he slumped into a sitting position against the wall and smiled foolishly as he died . . .

There was no smile on Bo Rangle's face, as from the cover of a doorway, he sent a bright tracer of lead screaming at the stairway and realized it was now one against one. He was confident he could beat the dude, even if he was one hell of a lead-slinger. But dare he linger to prove it, with sounds of the shots rolling far and wide out over the rooftops of Daybreak. . . the town that hated him and had driven him away. . .

The answer was no. Maybe he'd been reckless to come in here by daylight in the first place, but to waste another ten seconds now would be suicidal.

Consoling himself with a secret vow to level the score with that gunslick some way, somehow, Rangle triggered twice more through the twisting tendrils of gunsmoke and dashed for the rear balcony.

Benedict heard the thudding steps, sprang to his feet and sped down the hallway, leaping Matt Dunstan's faceless corpse. By the time he reached the gallery, Rangle had jumped to the ground below, landed with the agility of a puma and was dashing across the yard for the horses, long coat flapping wildly behind him.

Benedict fired and knew right away he'd shot too fast. At the air whip of the bullet fanning his cheek, Bo Rangle spun on high heels and set two shots snarling back. One took a fist-sized chunk of timber out of the balcony railing, the second creased the side of Benedict's skull.

The impact of the glancing blow drove Benedict spinning backward into the doorway, guns thumping loudly to the boards. He fell headlong, heard Belle Shilleen scream as she came rushing out. . .and the moment before blackness, the rapid stutter of Bo Rangle's horse carrying him away.

Hank Brazos had a distinct feeling that he'd been through all this before as he headed for Buck Tanner's livery by the sickly light of the next day's dawn.

Yesterday on quitting the bordello after Belle had dropped the hint where they might look for Bo Rangle, he'd come to the livery, fed Bullpup, saddled up the appaloosa and was all ready to haul his freight and get a head-start on the tardy Benedict. He'd been actually mounting up when the guns had started up from the direction of Belle's. By the time he'd reached the bordello, Bo Rangle was just a dusty speck in the distance, and upstairs in the passageway that looked more like a slaughterhouse, Belle was sobbing over Benedict quite sure he was dead.

Brazos had been sure too for a bad moment, until he took a closer look at the Yank and found out that he was only creased. Even so he didn't really breathe easy for well over an hour when Benedict came conscious under

Doc Murphy's care, and by then Rangle was to hell and gone.

Brazos had lazed around the hotel all that day while the Yank lay up in his room, ministered to by Belle and some of her girls. It had been a long, dull day and he'd gone to bed early, still believing he would wait for Benedict to recover before taking the trail.

But that had been last night. This morning he'd awakened very early to the realization that he was being a fool. Benedict surely wouldn't wait for him if their positions had been reversed. After all, it was Benedict himself who preached the gospel of looking out for Number One.

He reached the stables, went in and turned up the night light. Bullpup expected a little affection after several days of neglect, but had to be content with a quick cuff around the ears.

It took him only minutes to saddle up and get his warbag lashed into place. Yet even as he was buckling up the last cinch strap, Bullpup growled and a footfall sounded outside.

Brazos' eyes snapped wide with surprise. 'Yank!'

Benedict stood there against the gray sheen of the dawn sky, feet planted wide. He was fully dressed and had his warbag over his shoulder. He still wore the dressing the medic had put around his head, and his face was several shades paler than normal. Even so he looked tolerably healthy and tolerably unfriendly.

His expression a mixture of surprise and embarrassment, Brazos scratched his head, fidgeted, then said, 'Why. . . why it's sure nice to see you up and about so soon, Yank.'

Benedict walked in slowly, staring at the saddled horse. He dumped his warbag against the wall of a stall, tugged out his cigar case and cocked a sardonic eyebrow.

'You wouldn't be thinking of riding off without me by any chance, would you, Johnny Reb?'

'Hell no, Yank,' Brazos said as if that was about the last thing he would have thought of. 'No, I was just saddlin' up for an early-mornin' ride.' He patted the appaloosa. 'He's packin' on fat standin' around here doin' nothin' but work his way through a dollar's worth of chaff a day.'

'Oh sure, sure. And the warbag's just to add a little extra weight and help run off the fat. Right?'

Brazos sighed. He was a poor liar. He grinned, then he scowled.

It was finally Benedict who broke the uncomfortable silence.

'Well, Reb, how do we play the game? We both want the gold, but we don't mean to share it. And now, we both know where to start looking. So what do we do? Ride separate trails and maybe end up trying to kill one another, or do we ride together, at least until we find out if there is any gold?'

Brazos looked ferocious, the way he always looked when he was trying to figure something out.

Finally he said, 'The way I see it, Yank, if that gold is still about, then it ain't goin' to be easy to get hold of it, not when it's in Bo Rangle's hands, and with half the law of Missouri tryin' to take it off him.' He shook his head. 'Too big a job for one man, Benedict, and likely too big a job for two.' Then he grinned. 'But I reckon two would have twice the chance of one. What do you say?'

'I say I think it could work. We made a good team at Pea Ridge, Reb, and we've made a tolerably good team here.' The wide smile flashed as he extended his hand. 'I say we ride together.'

Brazos' big hand wrapped around his. 'No double-crossin' and no dealin' from the bottom of the deck until we've got that gold, Yank.' A pause, then, 'But the day we do find it, I guess it's a case of every man for himself.'

'Why,' Benedict smiled. 'I couldn't have said that better myself, Reb.' He bent and hefted his saddle gear. 'OK, let's get moving, we've got long miles to go.' They rode out together in brilliant sunshine with Bullpup swaggering along behind and farewell handkerchiefs fluttering from the upper balcony of Belle Shilleen's. They'd come to this dusty little Kansas cowtown by separate ways, one driven by gold-fever and ambition, the other by nothing more than wanderlust. Now they left together as partners.

But partners for how long? Surely not much farther beyond the first opportunity either saw to double-cross the other?

So it would seem . . . and yet unsuspected by anybody, least of all the two men concerned, that wary handshake in a dusty livery stable in Daybreak, Kansas, was destined to be the foundation of an unlikely partnership that Destiny decreed would grow strong in time, strong enough to weather a thousand shared dangers, to survive ten thousand violent miles, and ultimately, over the years, to become a stirring chapter in the living legends of the West.